A GRAVE DECISION

"Hold it, Bob," Lucky said. "This young bastard's killed a lot of men. They say he's fast and cold-blooded."

"He don't look cold-blooded."

"Well, that's what they say."

Bob studied Cuno with renewed interest, cocking his head to one side and slitting his eyes. He winced and chewed his lower lip. "He don't look so tough to me. Lucky, do you realize that if we took this shavetail down and collected that five thousand, we wouldn't have to brush-pop beef for pennies and piss water for a good long time?"

"I realize that. But I also realize we can't collect the five thousand if we're pushin' up sod."

Cuno smiled tightly. "I don't think Lucky's feeling so lucky, Bob. Maybe you better listen to him."

PETER BRANDVOLD IS ...

D0836736

.45-CALIBER MANHUNT

PETER BRANDVOLD

BERKLEY BOOKS, NEW YORK

THE BERKLEY PUBLISHING GROUP
Published by the Penguin Group
Penguin Group (USA) Inc.
375 Hudson Street, New York, New York 10014, USA

Penguin Group (Canada), 90 Eglinton Avenue East, Suite 700, Toronto, Ontario M4P 2Y3, Canada
(a division of Pearson Penguin Canada Inc.)
Penguin Books Ltd., 80 Strand, London WC2R 0RL, England
Penguin Group Ireland, 25 St. Stephen's Green, Dublin 2, Ireland (a division of Penguin Books Ltd.)
Penguin Group (Australia), 250 Camberwell Road, Camberwell, Victoria 3124, Australia
(a division of Pearson Australia Group Pty. Ltd.)
Penguin Books India Pvt. Ltd., 11 Community Centre, Panchsheel Park, New Delhi—110 017, India
Penguin Group (NZ), Cnr. Airborne and Rosedale Roads, Albany, Auckland 1310, New Zealand
(a division of Pearson New Zealand Ltd.)
Penguin Books (South Africa) (Pty.) Ltd., 24 Sturdee Avenue, Rosebank, Johannesburg 2196,
South Africa

Penguin Books Ltd., Registered Offices: 80 Strand, London WC2R 0RL, England

This is a work of fiction. Names, characters, places, and incidents either are the product of the author's imagination or are used fictitiously, and any resemblance to actual persons, living or dead, business establishments, events, or locales is entirely coincidental. The publisher does not have any control over and does not assume any responsibility for author or third-party websites or their content.

.45-CALIBER MANHUNT

A Berkley Book / published by arrangement with the author

PRINTING HISTORY
Berkley edition / February 2006

Copyright © 2006 by Peter Brandvold.

ISBN: 0-425-20845-1

BERKLEY®
Berkley Books are published by The Berkley Publishing Group,
a division of Penguin Group (USA) Inc.,
375 Hudson Street, New York, New York 10014.
BERKLEY is a registered trademark of Penguin Group (USA) Inc.
The "B" design is a trademark belonging to Penguin Group (USA) Inc.

PRINTED IN THE UNITED STATES OF AMERICA

10 9 8 7 6 5 4 3 2 1

For the North Country caballeros,
Kent Quammie and Jay Johnson

1

A GIANT IN a molted bearskin tunic lumbered through the tavern's louvered doors and stopped, fingering the sawed-off Winchester holstered on his waist and gazing around the saloon like a bear sniffing out a trash heap. In his left hand he clutched the tied top of a bloody burlap sack.

Finally, when his eyes had adjusted to the shadows, the giant cuffed the battered sombrero off his forehead, turned, and stalked up to the bar.

He was easily the biggest man in the saloon, one of the biggest who'd *ever* been in the saloon. He stood nearly seven feet tall without his hat or his stovepipe boots, and he was broader than the tables at which the handful of cowboys and freighters sat, eyeing the newcomer dubiously. His boots clapped like thunder, his spurs chinging raucously. Several of the men winced and blinked against his stench, which was like that of a recently vacated bear cave.

The giant dropped his bloody sack on the floor with a thump and stared dully at the bartender standing across from him. The man gazed up at the giant, his waxed mustache twitching.

"Back in town already, Ruben?" he asked bitterly.

"Gimme a drink," the big man grunted.

The bartender flushed. His voice was halting. "S-sorry, Ruben. You'll have to show some coins first."

The big man stared down at the barman dully, wrinkling his nose.

"Sorry, Ruben," the barman said again. He swallowed. "Those are the orders Mr. Belmont give me. 'If Ruben Pacheca can't pay for his drink when said drink is served, he ain't served.' Those were his exact words." The man spread his pale hands acquiescently. They trembled slightly.

Ruben Pacheca scowled at the bartender, mulling it over. Nearly the entire right side of his face was covered with a deep-red birthmark, which ended in a delicate swirl above his right eye. His beard on that side of his face was alkali-white, while the rest was sandy brown. His colorless eyes were set deep beneath a mantling ridge.

The room was so quiet that a whore could be heard moaning with false passion in a back-alley crib. All eyes were on Pacheca.

Finally, the giant grumbled, leaned down, and swung his bloody sack onto the counter with a dull thud.

"Good Lord!" the barman cried, stumbling back, slitting his eyes and shaking his head against the stench. "What the hell is that?"

With his two massive, brown hands, Pacheca unknotted the rope tying the sack closed. "This here," he said, pausing dramatically as he reached inside, "is Lester Hardison." He pulled his hand back out of the bag. The entire room gasped when it saw him clutching a human head by its hair.

He set the head on the bar. It sat there, droop-eyed, tilted, the tip of its tongue protruding from the pink slash of its mouth, like the head of a vandalized statue. Its off-white, blue-mottled pallor was like marble. Only the clotted, purple blood at the throat, where the head had been hastily sawed from the torso, betrayed the fact that the object had three days ago been riding the shoulders of a living, breathing man. A round, steel-gray hole shone just above the right eye, swelling that eye grotesquely from its socket.

And of course there was the smell. . . .

"Oh . . . my . . . *God*, Ruben," the bartender cried, leaning away and regarding the grisly sight with horror, "what in the hell do you think you're doing?"

"You know how much Lester Hardison's head is worth up in Blanchard, where he forced that priest to diddle them two nuns, then killed all three? After he robbed that stage and was on the run from the posse?"

The bounty hunter stared at the barman as though expecting an answer. The barman only stared at the grisly object on his recently polished bar, his skin bleached the same shade as Hardison's head.

"Seven hundred dollars," Pacheca finally said with a self-satisfied air, his voice rumbling like a train through a long tunnel. "Soon as I turn ole Lester in, I'll send ye what I owe ye."

Sheriff Will-John Sneed was standing outside his jailhouse, gazing at the saloon that the giant bounty hunter had just entered after leaving his buckskin stallion tied at the hitching post. Agitated, Sneed sniffed and spit and hitched his gun belt higher on his waist. He was twenty-six and new to the sheriff's job, having been a deputy for three years before the previous sheriff died of a heart stroke in his outhouse.

"I told that bastard I didn't wanna see him in my town again," Sneed said to the deputy standing beside him.

Earl Watts was only a year younger than Sneed and had been riding shotgun for the Overland Stage Company before his cousin, Sneed, had coaxed him into taking the deputy's job. Both men had grown up on hardscrabble farms in the Texas Panhandle. Like Sneed, Watts was a big, capable-looking man. He patrolled the town with a sawed-off shotgun he carried in a leather lanyard around his neck.

"You reckon we need to talk to him a little louder this

time?" Watts asked his cousin, his thin lips stretching into a cool smile.

"I reckon," Sneed said with an exaggerated sigh.

Alamosa had been quiet of late, since the trail herds had thinned. Too quiet for Sneed, who enjoyed the authority of his new position and had grown fond of wielding it. Having power to wield made a man like Sneed, who'd grown up poor and powerless, downright euphoric.

The only problem was that, in their euphoria, Sneed and Watts had cleaned up the town so quickly and so well that their jobs had grown dull.

"I reckon," Sneed repeated, spitting a stream of chew into the sifting dust of a passing freight wagon, "that ole bounty hunter needs his ears cleaned for him." He glanced at Watts. "Ready to do some cleanin'?"

"Cousin," Watts said, breaking open his shotgun and gazing at the two fresh wads in the bores, "I was born ready."

"All right, then," Sneed said, slapping the revolver strapped to his thigh and starting across the street.

The two men were only a few feet from the opposite boardwalk when two young ladies stepped out of the millinery shop beside the saloon. Each carried a small hatbox and a parasol. One was blond, the other brunette. Silky ringlets sprang about the shoulders of their ruffled calico dresses. Seeing the lawmen with their shiny badges, the girls paused on the boardwalk, twirling their parasols coquettishly.

"Hello there, Sheriff Sneed," the blonde said through an impossibly white smile. She threw her shoulders back, her chest out. Her dress, buttoned to her throat, revealed nothing but a slight swell.

Sneed and Watts paused before the boardwalk, returning the girls' smiles. Sneed lifted his hat and dropped it back on his head. "Miss Polly, Miss Sarah, nice to see you pretty ladies on this delightful afternoon."

Snorting, Watts elbowed Sneed in the ribs.

"It's nice to see you," the blonde returned as she stared smokily into the lawman's eyes, batting her lids. Canting her head onto a shoulder and giving the parasol a spin, she said, "You gonna be too busy to drop by the house tonight, Sheriff . . . for some lemonade?"

"Oh, I reckon I can find an hour to spare," Sneed said, scratching the back of his head. "Or maybe even two, if you're sure it's all right with your folks . . ."

"Oh, it's more than all right, Sheriff," the blonde assured. "Why, Papa says if you can't trust a lawman with your daughter, who can you trust her with?" The smile widened, flashing nearly the whole set of perfect teeth behind the full, cherry lips.

Watts snickered and again elbowed Sneed. Staring at those lips, Sneed felt the prick of desire in his loins.

With a self-satisfied chuckle, he said, "Well, your papa sure has that right. You're in safe hands when I'm around, Miss Polly. None safer."

In Sneed's mind flashed the image from two nights ago, of the girl undressing in her father's woodshed while their glasses of iced lemonade warmed on the porch. Naked, she'd propped herself back against the pile of neatly split and stacked oak, apple, and box elder. Sneed had dropped his jeans to his ankles and was thrusting between the girl's creamy thighs, white as fresh milk in the moonlight filtering through the cracks between the logs. He'd clamped one hand over her mouth to keep her moans from her grayheaded father, Alamosa's most prominent businessman. She'd bucked against Sneed like a wild filly breaking for the hills.

They'd just returned to their lemonade, flushed and exhausted, when the girl's mother had appeared, chortling that it was Polly's bedtime. . . .

Now the girl tittered and shot a glance at the brunette. "Isn't he just a peach?" she asked.

"Indeed he is," the brunette agreed, favoring Alamosa's new sheriff with a meaningful glance of her own.

"Well, Miss Polly, Miss Sarah," Sneed said, his countenance turning serious, "my deputy and I have some business to tend in the Prairie Fire. We wouldn't want you gettin' hurt, so I suggest you both run along home to your quilt-work an' such."

The girls' bright smiles quickly turned to wary frowns. "Is it serious trouble, Sheriff?" Polly asked.

"Serious enough," Sneed said with a grave dip of his chin, "but nothing my deputy and I can't handle. We wouldn't want any innocent bystanders gettin' hurt, so . . ."

"Oh, yes." Shifting her parcel, Miss Polly grabbed Miss Sarah's wrist. Furling her brows gravely, she said, "We'll get out of your way and let you lawmen do your jobs. Come along, Sarah."

The girls hurried off down the boardwalk. Miss Polly stopped suddenly and cast a concerned look behind her. "Do be careful, Sheriff."

Sneed touched his hat to the girl and turned away, his expression somber as he mounted the boardwalk. Watts sidled up to him, in a thin voice mocking, "Do be careful, Sheriff. . . . Don't hurt nothin' I'll be needin' tonight. . . ."

"You're so jealous you could choke a shoat with it." Sneed snickered as he approached the saloon, one hand on his revolver's butt.

He pushed through the batwings, took two steps, and stopped. As Watts walked up beside him, Sneed looked around the dimly lit room. Seven or eight cowboys and freighters sat here and there before soapy beer mugs, quieter even than usual for this time of the day.

Several customers glanced at the two lawmen meaningfully, then shuttled their gazes to the bar, where the big bounty hunter stood with a bottle and a shot glass. Sneed's gaze held on the grisly object sitting beside the Old Crow bottle, a shock of auburn hair winging down around the head's bulging right eye.

The sheriff's breath caught in his throat, and his stomach soured. It took him several seconds to find his voice. Then, scrunching his face with disbelief, he said, "Dog my cats, Ruben! What in the hell is that?"

The giant in the buffalo tunic turned his ugly face to the sheriff. He stood sideways at the bar, facing the front window, his left elbow on the mahogany. He held his shot glass in his right hand. The butt of his sawed-off rifle jutted up near his wrist.

Ruben Pacheca nodded at the head, his birthmark turning a deeper shade of crimson as he beamed through the white beard on that side of his face. "That there's Lester Hardison. That there's my winter poke." Pacheca's shoulders bobbed as he wheezed a laugh from deep in his chest. "Didn't see no reason to haul his whole body in and fag a good horse!"

The massive shoulders bobbed again.

His face still scrunched up with incredulity, Sneed walked heavy-footed toward the giant. His gaze was glued to the head. He stopped a few feet away from it. Swallowing bile sent up by his churning stomach, Sneed extended an arm, pointing.

"That ain't Lester Hardison, you cork-headed hickernut! That's Bill Thornbush, ramrod of the T-Bar Ranch!"

The bartender was standing several yards away, his back to the back bar's mirror. "Jesus God, I thought he looked familiar!"

Pacheca looked at the head, furrowing his brows. Skeptically, he said, "That ain't Hardison?"

"No, it ain't Hardison!"

"Sure, it is."

"It's Bill Thornbush!"

Pacheca stared at the head. "It sure looks like Hardison. And he sure didn't deny it." He scrubbed his beard with a meaty paw. "But then, I reckon I didn't give him a whole lot of time. . . ."

"Where'd you run into him?" Watts asked. He'd come up behind the bounty hunter, his shotgun raised, both rabbit-eared hammers thumbed back.

"Up along the trail to Del Norte."

Sneed nodded. "That's T-Bar country, you fool. And that there is Bill Thornbush, one of the most respected ramrods in the Southwest. Why, he rode for Goodnight and Ed Bassingdale!"

Pacheca glanced at the head again. Damn—there went the reward money. Fingering his chin whiskers pensively, he turned to Sneed. "Well, hell, it was an honest mistake!"

Sneed drew his Colt and ratcheted back the hammer. "I told you to stay clear of my town, you wild-assed old lummox. Now, here you are, totin' Bill Thornbush's head." Sneed glanced at Watts standing behind Pacheca, shotgun raised to his shoulder and aimed at the giant's head. "Now, I reckon you'll be here till the circuit judge rolls through and arranges a necktie party. Then you'll be outta my hair fer good."

Sneed raised his Colt threateningly. "Lift those hands high above your head, Ruben, and I mean high!"

Pacheca just stared at him for several seconds. Then he glanced at Watts behind him. Seeing the two wide bores of the shotgun yawning at his head, he snorted disgustedly, set his shot glass on the bar, and raised his hands.

"Higher!" Sneed shouted.

Again, Pacheca just stared at him, pondering a move. Deciding it wouldn't work—not with that barn-blaster bearing down on him from behind—he snorted and raised his hands above his head, till his fingers brushed the ceiling.

Watts leaned forward and, holding his shotgun with his right hand, removed Pacheca's sawed-off rifle from its custom-made holster with his left. When Watts had set the rifle on the bar a good ways away from Pacheca, Sneed reached inside the giant's tunic and, squinting against the smell of the man, removed a Colt Navy from a shoulder holster. When he'd removed a Green River knife from a belt sheath and a .36 pocket pistol and an Arkansas tooth-pick from the man's right boot, Sneed backed away, his Colt raised at the giant's forehead.

"You got any more weapons, we'll find 'em when we strip ye down in the jailhouse."

"You ain't strippin' me, ye faggot!" Pacheca growled, puffing his jowls like an enraged cur.

Soft laughter rose from several tables, which had up to now been graveyard silent.

Sneed wagged the pistol, indicating the batwings. "Move your ass!"

Pacheca hemmed and hawed and finally lumbered, cursing, across the room and through the batwings. Watts followed him out.

Pausing before the doors, Sneed turned to the bartender. "Ray, put Thornbush's head in the sack and bring it over to the jailhouse." Turning to one of the customers, he said, "Junior, gather up his weapons."

The bartender flushed with exasperation. "I ain't touchin' that thing!"

"You bring it over, you hear?" Sneed said with a threatening look.

"Ah, Jesus!" the bartender said, turning his pained gaze to Thornbush's head staring sleepily across the saloon, where the customers sat in a churchly hush.

"That's more like it," Sneed said, and went out.

When he and Watts had followed Pacheca over to the jailhouse, he ordered the giant to stop a few feet before the door. Telling Watts to keep his shotgun on the bounty man's back, Sneed walked around front and opened the door.

"Now get in there and get your clothes off," Sneed ordered the prisoner, stepping aside to let him pass through the door.

"I told you," Pacheca boomed as he ducked through the door frame, "you faggots try undressin' me, you're gonna be wearin' your tin stars on your foreheads!"

"Haul your ass, you son of a bitch!" Watts ordered, lifting his shotgun high and planting the butt between the giant's shoulder blades, sending him stumbling into the jailhouse.

Watts turned to Sneed, grinning. "Hear that, Will-John? The big bastard's gonna pin our stars to our foreheads."

"Ouch!" Sneed said, rubbing his temple as he turned through the door. "That'd hurt somethin' serious!"

Guffawing, Watts followed the sheriff inside and slammed the door behind him. A few minutes later, the reluctant bartender brought the head over in its bloody burlap sack, followed by the man named Junior carrying the bounty hunter's guns and knives. The men made their deliveries and hurried back to the saloon, jogging past the bounty hunter's horse still tethered to the hitching post.

Fifteen minutes later, the jailhouse door opened about two feet. Pacheca poked his head out, glancing first one way down the street and then the other.

Seeing that the street was clear, the town quiet, the big man stepped outside, drew the door closed behind him, and strode across the street to his horse. His sawed-off Winchester jutted up from the custom-made holster belted around his bearskin tunic.

Casual, unhurried, Pacheca turned a stirrup out and swung his bulky frame into the saddle. The leather creaked, and the horse braced itself under the massive weight of its rider.

Whistling softly, the bounty hunter reined away from the hitch rack. He paused, took another look around. Still seeing no one, he gigged the big buckskin into an easy jog, heading north past the tool store and the blacksmith shop. He rode loosely, arms high, chin up, like a man heading home, tired but proud, after a hard day's work.

When the last of the town's shanties and the old stage station had passed away behind him, he gigged the buckskin into a canter, and broke into rhythmless song:

> *I once knew a filly from Abil-eene.*
> *I tell you, gents, that girl would buck and bounce*
>   *like a* queen—!

After another verse, Ruben Pacheca rounded the bend past the lightning-split cedar, and was gone.

Only minutes later, Miss Polly and Miss Sarah stepped out from the alley between the millinery and the saddle shop. Giggling and speaking in hushed voices, they angled across the street toward the jailhouse. Miss Polly carried a plate of freshly baked cookies in both hands, beaming and shy.

Pausing before the closed jailhouse door, Polly turned to Sarah. "You don't think I'm being too forward, do you?"

Sarah tittered. "How could you be any more forward than you've already been!"

Polly pursed her lips. "Good point." She gave the door a cursory knock, turned the knob, and threw it open.

Both girls froze in the doorway. The plate tumbled from Polly's hands, crashing to the floor, shattering, sending cookies and china shards flying. Slapping their hands to their mouths, the girls screamed. Polly jumped back into Sarah, and the two girls tumbled over the door frame on their butts, skirts and petticoats twirling about buffeting bloomers.

Clawing at each other and at the hitch rack, the girls clambered to their feet, the volume and pitch of their screams rising with each seizure. Their faces were flushed, twisted, and swollen with bald, heartrending terror.

Forgetting their feminine training, they sprinted across the street like boys, elbows pumping, knees driving. Halfway across the street, Sarah slipped in fresh horse apples and fell hard on her forearms. Polly didn't slow in the least. When she reached the alley between the millinery and the saddle shop, she was gone, her screams echoing behind her.

"Good Lord, what in the hell was that all about?" exclaimed Ray McCarthy, the Prairie Fire's bartender, as he pushed through the batwings with a surprised look on his face. He was holding the beer mug and towel he'd been holding when he'd heard the screams. He gazed into the street.

Crying uncontrollably, Miss Sarah had climbed to her feet and was scampering around the corner of the millinery shop, disappearing down the alley. As the afternoon drinkers stumbled out behind the barman, squinting against the sun glare, several carrying their beers, Ray McCarthy turned his curious gaze to the jailhouse's open door.

Frowning, he shoved the glass and the towel at the nearest

customer, and headed across the street. Several men trailed him at a distance, looking around as though the town were being attacked by Indians. Several shopkeepers had appeared from their stores and were slowly heading this way, faces lined with worry.

As Ray McCarthy approached the jailhouse, he called through the door, "Sneed . . . Watts . . . you men in there?"

Blinking his eyes and staring into the room's dense shadows, McCarthy stepped over the threshhold and stopped suddenly. His mouth slowly opened, as though under the power of a building scream.

Before him, on a battered desk facing the door, sat the severed, gaping heads of Sheriff Sneed and Deputy Watts, their five-pointed stars pinned to their bloody foreheads.

A mile beyond the town, Ruben Pacheca reined his buckskin to a halt. The massive bounty hunter fished a folded paper from the inside breast pocket of his tunic. He opened the sheet carefully and held it out, frowning.

He'd found the sheet pinned to the bulletin board in Sneed's office. It read:

**WANTED
DEAD OR ALIVE
Cuno Massey
FOR THE COLD-BLOODED MURDER
OF VINCE EVANS OF JULESBURG:
$5,000**

Pacheca scrutinized the sketch of the young man included on the dodger, then refolded the sheet and stuffed it back in his pocket. He gave a long whistle and shook his head, impressed by the amount of the bounty.

"Come on, Animal," he told the horse, gigging the buckskin up the trail, heading north. "Let's make some money."

2

IN THE QUIET night, a twig snapped.

Cuno Massey came instantly awake, throwing his single blanket aside while reaching for the Frontier Colt in the holster and gun belt coiled on the ground beside him. He cleared leather and thumbed the hammer back.

The hammer's scrape disturbed the boy sleeping to Cuno's right. Curled on his side, head on his saddle, Sandy Hilman gave a start, jerking his shoulders and tossing his head. Then the boy relaxed with a quiet groan, and he was sleeping again.

Cuno sat up, staring tensely across the umber glow of the dying campfire, listening. The noise could have marked only the passing of some night predator searching for four-legged prey. But it could also have signaled the approach of some two-legged predator searching for two-legged prey.

When you had a two-thousand-dollar bounty on your head, you couldn't sleep too lightly. Many times over the past year, since he'd killed the son of a prominent rancher, men had come gunning for him. It seemed the more who came and the more he killed, the more who swarmed to the challenge, wanting to make a name for themselves as the killer of Cuno Massey. A gang of such men—the Hudson Gang—had killed his young wife, July, while trying to kill him.

July had given him hope and a reason to go on living after his parents had been brutally murdered. To have her murdered, too, was more horror and heartbreak than he thought he'd ever have to endure.

That's why he was heading north—to settle the score with Franklin Evans, the man who'd put the price on his head, sicced the bounty hunters on him, and caused the murder of Cuno's beloved July.

But there would be no starting over until the bounty was off his head.

To his left, something rustled in the underbrush. An alarm clanged in his brain, and he flung his right arm at the boy, gently but urgently shaking Sandy's shoulder.

"Come on," he whispered. "Wake up."

They had been together for several weeks now, and the boy had acquired a calm awareness. He lifted his head, coming instantly awake, blinking his eyes but saying nothing.

Cuno enunciated each word softly and carefully. "Move out from the camp. Take your gun. Hide in the brush and don't come out till I say."

Silently, the boy reached for his revolver—a Remington Cuno had removed from the carcass of one of the men who had killed his wife—and rolled out from beneath his blankets, stealing away in the brush.

Moving in the opposite direction, Cuno did likewise, padding in his stocking feet through the shrubs, along a game trail, and crouching behind a mossy boulder. He looked around. The dime-sized moon was bright, and silhouettes humped around him. The black columns of trees jutted above the shrubs and boulders of this ancient riverbed.

There was very little movement—only a slender branch nudged by a vagrant breeze, fallen leaves through which a tiny night creature burrowed. An owl hooted.

There was a rustle, quiet but louder than any of the other night sounds.

Cuno turned his head to his left in time to see a shadow slip behind a double-trunked tree silhouetted against the milky sky. He holstered his revolver, palmed his razor-edged bowie, and started toward the cottonwood, his feet making no more noise than an Indian's. Approaching the tree, he moved around the left side of the wide trunk until he saw the man standing behind it.

Crouching, his back to Cuno and holding a rifle in both hands, the man gazed through the thick shrubs toward the camp where Cuno and the boy had been sleeping.

Cuno eased forward until he could see the rise and fall of the man's shoulders as he breathed, hear his raspy breath. Cuno lunged, wrapping his left hand around the man's mouth and jerking him back against the knife point, then heaving the blade deep into the man's back, working it through the ribs and angling it up toward the heart.

Thick, hot blood washed over Cuno's wrist. The man grunted through Cuno's taut fingers, struggled violently for a moment, then slowly relaxed, knees sagging.

Cuno grabbed the rifle before the man could drop it, carefully lowered the gun and the man to the ground, giving his hand and knife a hasty wipe on the dead man's denims.

Someone whistled. Cuno froze and looked around. A shadow moved in the shrubs thirty yards before him, then stopped—a stooped, bulky figure, moonlight gleaming off the barrel of the revolver in the man's hands.

The man stood staring, not sure whom he was staring at. Cuno stared back, his heart thudding.

Seconds ticked by, slow and plodding. Cuno sensed the man's indecision.

Finally, the man jerked, the gun flashing as it rose. Cuno clawed his own Colt and fired, blowing the night wide-open and throwing the man back into the shrubs with a grunt and a rustle and the crunch of broken branches.

Silence.

Cuno's gun smoke thinned toward the stars.

"Dell?" someone called from Cuno's right and about twenty yards ahead.

Cuno fired two quick shots at a moving branch. When he heard a cry, he stepped back behind the tree, pivoting in time to see another man appear behind him—a big, broad-shouldered man in a rakishly cocked hat.

"Hey!" the man yelled, lowering a carbine.

He fired at the same time Cuno did, his slug chewing a piece from the tree with an angry plunk. Cuno's slug jerked the man back and to his left with an angry curse. He dropped to a knee, holding his left arm straight down at his side. One-handed, he began lifting the rifle again.

But he got it only half raised when Cuno fired twice more, methodically placing two more holes in the man's chest and head and throwing him back and sideways, silencing him forever. The rifle spun away, glanced off a boulder, and landed with a clatter.

Cuno heard a horse blow and stomp behind him. Spinning, he ran, replacing his Colt's spent shells with fresh as he ducked through the brush.

As he slammed the loading gate closed, hooves thundered to his right. In the darkness the silhouette of a horse and a rider swelled as it galloped toward him.

Cuno spun and leapt as the rider fired two shots. One slug spanged off a rock; the other raked a four-inch swath of skin from Cuno's left hand as he rolled off his shoulder and came up firing.

His first two shots sailed wide of the figure retreating through the woods, heading north. The third caused the rider to flinch. The fourth blew him forward over his horse's head, somersaulting him through the air as the horse, screaming, followed the rider to the ground in a flurry of flapping stirrups and scissoring hooves.

The horse got up, its saddle hanging down one side, and shook. It trotted off through the brush, snorting and shaking its head.

The rider stayed down, a dark figure rolling from side to

side and moaning from deep in his chest. His Colt hanging down at his thigh, Cuno walked over to the would-be ambusher and looked down.

The man's hat had fallen off. He was bald except for a strap of hair just above his jug ears. He wore a fringed deer-hide jacket dyed red, and a striped shirt, which was bloody around the right shoulder. He was long and lean and savage-faced. His teeth glistened white in the moonlight as he snarled like a trapped coyote.

His eyes finding Cuno staring coolly down at him, he spit a string of epithets through vise-tight jaws. Cuno recognized him. He'd been a part of a gang playing poker in the saloon back in Muddy Flats, the little mining town through which Cuno and the boy had passed two days before.

Cuno squatted over the man and said levelly, "Mister, there ain't enough reward money in the world worth dyin' for."

The wounded man winced as pain stabbed him. Sneering, he said, "There's five thousand on you now, boy. Old Evans upped the ante." He slid his right hand toward the revolver holstered on his thigh. "I've taken bigger risks for less."

Cuno watched the hand. As it began sliding the gun from the holster, Cuno lifted his own revolver and stopped the slide of the man's hand with a bullet through his brain plate, clouding both eyes with instant death. The man's chin dropped and turned; his fists tightened, then relaxed.

Still holding his smoking Colt waist high, Cuno looked around, listening. Hearing nothing, he walked back toward the camp, keeping his revolver drawn and ready but holding it down near his thigh.

He stayed alert, but his thoughts drifted back to the night he'd killed Vince Evans in a Julesburg whorehouse. Hearing a girl scream, he'd run to the room and stared into the clutter lit by a single, red-shaded lamp.

On the bed were the whore named Minnie and a tall man with mussed, chestnut hair and long sideburns. He and

the girl were naked. The man knelt before Minnie, her back
to the wall, knees raised protectively to her chest. He had a
handful of her hair and was pulling her head back, expos-
ing her neck to the wide-bladed knife in his other hand.

Minnie said nothing. Her wide eyes were glazed with fear.

"Goddamn whore! I've had enough o' your sass!"

With that, he whipped the knife back, the tip pointed toward her exposed neck.

"Stop!" Cuno ordered Evans.

The man whipped his red-mottled face at him. His eyes
narrowed briefly at the gun in Cuno's hand. A grin pulled
at the man's mouth, and he whipped back toward Minnie,
thrusting the knife toward her throat.

His arm's forward motion had just started when Cuno's
Colt bucked, spitting smoke and flames. The bullet carved
a neat hole through Evans's head, just above his ear, and
the tall man flew over Minnie and into the wall, folding up
on the bed like a pile of white laundry.

Now Cuno shook his head and kicked a stone. All this
killing because some whore riled a spoiled rancher's son to a
murderous fury. Vince Evans's father, a prominent Julesburg
rancher, had promptly issued a bounty on Cuno's head.
From the rumors Cuno had heard lately, the man had con-
vinced everyone that Cuno had killed Vince in cold blood.

So now he had not only bounty hunters on his trail, but
lawmen, as well.

Five thousand dollars . . .

He stopped by the near-dead fire. "Boy?"

The shrubs across the fire moved.

"Here," came the twelve-year-old's reply. Sandy Hilman
stepped out from the shrubs, eyes wide with expectation
and curiosity, his hair and shirt still rumpled from sleep.
In his right hand hung the heavy Remington. Like Cuno,
he was still in his stocking feet.

At Cuno's side these past several weeks, he'd become
far too familiar with blood and death. He did not gulp or
tremble. Blandly, he asked, "Who were they?"

"Those five drovers from Muddy Flats." Cuno kicked

dirt on the fire. "Gather your gear. We're pulling out. No telling who or what that gunfire'll bring in."

Sandy Hilman nodded, and had started turning away when he stopped suddenly and turned back, staring wide-eyed over Cuno's right shoulder.

"Look out!"

Just before the boy had given his warning, Cuno had heard the brush rustle behind him. He dropped to his knees as a rifle exploded twenty yards away. He rolled off his hip and froze, his Colt in his hand. The slim outline of the gunman pivoted and bolted back through the shrubs.

Cuno whipped a fearful gaze at the boy, who had flung himself clear of the bullet's path. "Sandy, stay down!"

Cuno bolted after the retreating figure, his Colt in his right hand, his left arm raised to shield his face from branches. He jumped deadfalls, leapt stumps, and at the edge of the copse in which he and the boy had camped, he hurdled a shallow stream.

Ahead, the gunman ran with surprising speed, a flickering shadow heading across a grassy clearing bathed in silvery moonlight.

Topping a natural levee, Cuno stopped and raised the Colt. "Stop or take it in the back!"

The figure continued running, diminishing in the milky-dark distance.

Cuno flicked the Colt's hammer back and aimed, but for some reason his finger would not take up the trigger slack. Confused by his own reluctance to fire, he bolted forward once again, running hard, his left arm sawing like a piston as his muscled thighs propelled him through the tall grass, his navy neckerchief whipping his face, his heart and lungs working like those of a work-seasoned Percheron.

The slender figure grew before him until, near a dark strap of woods on the other side of the clearing, he was twenty yards away . . . then ten . . . five . . .

He flung himself into the running man. The two went down, rolling through the grass. Cuno bounded atop the gunman's back. He grabbed the man's shirt at the shoulders and flung him around with surprising ease. Buttons popped and the gunman's shirt flew open to reveal a pair of pert, pale female breasts loosely swathed in a man's torn undershirt and bathed lovingly in the glittering light of the kiting moon.

3

"WHAT THE . . . ?" CUNO said, sending his gaze northward from the open shirt. The girl glared up at him from a nest of mussed blond hair. "Who in the hell are you?"

"Get off me!" she raged, struggling against him. But her strength was no match for his. He pinned her flailing arms in the tall grass while he straddled her waist on his knees. She kicked at him feebly, grunting and snarling like a trapped animal. "Get off me, you son of a bitch!"

She managed to pull her right hand free and punched his jaw. She swung it back, recocking. He grabbed it again and pinned it down by her ear. The blow had stunned him, left what felt like a darning needle in his jaw. He gazed down at this strange, wolverinelike female, wanting to return the favor, but it was not in Cuno Massey's nature to strike a woman—even one who had tried to backshoot him.

"Settle down!" he yelled. She lifted her butt and twisted her waist, kicking at him feebly. It took every ounce of his own strength to keep her hands pinned to the ground.

"Get . . . off . . . me!"

"Pull your horns in!"

"I'll kill you, you murderin' bastard!"

"You already tried that. You're the ones out to murder me, remember? I was just defending myself."

"I know who you are—how many men you've killed!" she raged. Her right hand nearly slipped from his grasp again. He caught it and clamped it back down.

He was still struggling with the girl, thoroughly awed by her strength, when lace-up boots appeared in the grass beside him. Looking up, he saw the silhouette of the boy staring down at him. Cuno couldn't see Sandy's face, as the moon was behind the boy, but he imagined his thoughts as he watched Cuno, who stood just six feet tall and weighed nearly two hundred pounds, struggling with a girl a foot shorter and half his weight.

"Boy, I've got a viper here, and if she doesn't quit fightin' in three seconds, I'm gonna cut her damn throat!"

"You are?" Sandy sounded genuinely surprised.

"I sure as hell am," Cuno lied. "Because I'm a murderin' bastard!" He slid up higher on the girl's chest, till he was nearly straddling her exposed breasts. When he had her arms pinned under his knees, he unholstered his Colt, jammed the barrel against the girl's forehead, and thumbed the hammer back.

"Cuno, don't do it!" the boy cried.

"She's too damn much trouble," Cuno said.

The girl froze suddenly, tensing, her wide eyes staring up at Cuno from around the barrel of the pistol jammed against her forehead, an inch above her nose. She swallowed, her breath growing shallow.

"You want to die?" Cuno asked her.

Her body relaxed, and she lay inert beneath him. In the shadow his own body cast upon her, he saw that her bold, handsome face had bleached with fear.

Cuno stood, breathing hard. He kept his revolver on her, his eyes raking her body for more weapons. She appeared around eighteen. She wore tight blue jeans, a brown flannel shirt over a man's torn undershirt, and a blue neckerchief.

On her feet was a pair of men's overlarge cowboy boots, the pointed toes curling back upon themselves, like elf shoes.

She returned his appraising gaze, her lips set with anger and apprehension. She was a hellcat, this one, with a pretty, cunning face—high-boned, pale-skinned, with a splash of freckles across her nose and on both cheeks. Her pale blue eyes were like those of a cat, widely spaced and tilted slightly up at the corners. A pretty, beguiling polecat she was, with all the right curves in all the right places, but a she-cat who rode with dry-gulchers.

"What's your handle, girl?"

She lay staring up at him, making no move to rise but folding her arms across her chest and torn shirt, covering herself. "What's it to you?"

"You get smart, I'll plug you." He flicked the gun at her again and added, "Remember, I'm a murderin' bastard."

She opened her mouth to speak. Her breath caught. She cleared her throat. "Marlene Stratton."

"When did you start riding with bushwhackers, Marlene Stratton?"

She sniffed, lifted a hand to wipe her nose. "If you're gonna kill me, kill me, damn ye."

"Answer my question."

"Couple months ago."

"Who *were* they?"

"They all dead?"

"Yep."

Staring with newfound respect at the .45 Colt aimed at her head, she said, "Folks called us the Morgan Gang."

"Morgan?"

"Jess and Rocky Morgan were the leaders. They had a ranch south of here. We didn't spend much time there, though. Jess an' Rocky didn't much care for cows."

"How'd you happen to join up?"

Marlene Stratton sighed and said wearily, "I was slingin' hash in Alamosa an' Jess and some of the boys came in. Jess asked me out, and one thing led to another. . . ."

Cuno didn't say anything. He and Sandy stood on either side of her, staring down at her.

"We weren't so bad." Her voice acquired a defensive edge. "We just robbed stages and such. Never killed nobody. Mostly, I held the horses while the boys shook the passengers down."

"Why were you after me?"

The girl's catlike eyes hooded, impatient but at the same time regarding the bore of Cuno's Colt warily.

"Jess and the boys seen you in that roadhouse in Muddy Flats."

"They recognize me from a wanted dodger?"

She nodded.

Cuno curled his lip angrily. "So you decided to steer your careers in a different direction. . . ."

"We heard you had five thousand dollars on you," she said impatiently, as though trying to convince a dunderhead that two plus two equaled four.

Cuno thought about that. With a bounty that high, half the frontier would be on his ass.

"I didn't see you in Muddy Flats."

"I was tendin' the saddle stock." Her voice expressed a cool resentment as she added, "Like always . . ."

Cuno holstered his revolver and plucked her rifle out of the grass. It was a weathered, rusty Spencer.

She remained where she was. "If you're gonna kill me, I wish you'd just do it. The ground's hard, and I'm gettin' cold."

"Get up."

"What for?" she said suspiciously.

"Get up."

She raised up on her elbows. In the moonlight, her brows ridged. She glanced at Sandy, then returned her gaze to Cuno. "You ain't gonna ravage me in front of the boy, are you?"

Cuno snorted. "Not tonight." He ejected shells from the Spencer. They clanked together in the grass. "Get up."

She climbed to her feet slowly, keeping her gaze on Cuno.

"What am I supposed to do with you?" he said with disgust.

She held his gaze with an air of defiance, her arms across her breasts. "Kill me, I guess, like you did the others."

Cuno canted his head at her. "Where you from, Marlene?"

She shrugged. "Nowhere, really. Wichita. After Ma ran off with a preacher, my pa turned outlaw, and I rode along."

Cuno studied her, amazed. She didn't look like an outlaw girl. She had an edge conveyed by the slanted blue eyes, but most outlaw women were ugly. "Suppose I let you go, what would you do?"

She shrugged. "Reckon I'd drift."

Cuno thought it over. Alone and without weapons, she wouldn't be much of a threat to him or the boy, but he might do her a bigger favor by shooting her. A girl alone out here, in Southern Cheyenne and Kiowa country, a country teeming with non-Indian renegades to boot, wouldn't have much of a chance.

"The boy and I'll try to run down a horse for you," Cuno said. "You can ride with us to the next town."

She squinted her eyes at him skeptically. "What for?"

"What do you mean, what for?"

"Why you bein' so charitable? I tried to kill you."

"Believe me," he said, "if you were a man, you'd be worm food with the others."

He turned, touched Sandy's shoulder, and the two began walking back toward their bivouac. "We'll break camp and saddle up."

Watching them walk away, the girl laughed caustically. "You think you can get money for me along the trail somewhere. No, thanks. I ain't no whore and I ain't no slave. I'll take my chances on my own."

"You got too much class for a whore, that it? Just screw murderers and thieves?"

"Kiss my ass, bucko."

"Have it your way."

"I usually do."

Cuno stopped and turned around. He studied her from a distance—a slender figure standing stiff with defiance against the stars.

Holding up the Spencer, he said, "I'll leave your rifle and shells near the fire. You can pick them up when we're gone." He turned and walked away, the boy following close on his heels.

Ten minutes later, they were trailing through the low pines, tracing a northeasterly path, slouched in their saddles. Moon filtering through the trees dappled the needle-covered ground. Cuno glanced at the boy, whose chin drooped sleepily as they traversed a low ridge stippled with prickly pear and bitter bush.

"Crazy life for a kid," Cuno grumbled, half to himself. "Dodging bounty hunters in the middle of the damn night."

"I don't mind it, Cuno."

"You don't mind livin' like a savage? Watching me kill?"

"I killed, too," Sandy said.

Cuno jerked his head sharply. He hadn't thought the boy remembered killing Marcella Jiminez, the gold-seeking whore who had pulled a gun on Cuno in the ghost town of Wild Horse a month ago. The boy had looked so dazed afterward, and had been so silent about it up to now, that Cuno had thought he'd blocked it out of his mind.

"I'm sorry about that, Sandy," he said now.

"Wasn't your fault."

"You were saving my hide. Because of me, you have blood on your hands."

Cuno couldn't tell if the killing bothered the boy or not. He hoped it did. Blood was often hard to wash off.

"We have to find you a home. A good family where you can grow up normal."

"I couldn't just stay with you, Cuno?"

"Staying with me ain't good for your health."

At first light, they halted their horses along a run-out spring, built a small fire, and made coffee. Cuno sipped a tin mug of the hot brew as he watched the sun rise over a

distant rimrock, painting the sky pink, then salmon, until
the sun was a bright, pulsing orb looming over the mountain. He rolled a smoke and enjoyed the quirley while the
air warmed and he surveyed the country through his field
glasses, looking for Indians and bounty hunters.

When he'd finished his quirley, he and Sandy mounted
up and headed north again through hills rolling up purple
with sage, the higher slopes stippled with piñons and ju-
nipers. Mid-morning, they came upon a pack of hungry
coyotes fighting over a dead deer in a dry wash below their
trail. The coyotes were in such a frenzy over the fresh kill
that they didn't even glance at the passing horsemen.

Later, Cuno and Sandy stopped at a roadhouse nestled
in a hollow between buttes. It was run by a wizened oldster
with a bald pink pate and a curly white beard. The stew was
a dime, the man told them, swinging an empty pail as he
returned from the hog pen. Coffee was an extra nickel.

Cuno and the boy were sitting at one of the two rough
benches, hungrily eating the antelope stew, when hooves
clomped outside. Cuno's horse, Renegade, whinnied a warning from the corral. Cuno leaned back from the table to peer
through the open door.

Three riders were entering the dusty, sunlit yard at a
walk. Between two men in rough trail garb rode a girl, her
blond hair ruffling in the breeze. She wore tight blue jeans,
a brown plaid shirt held closed with rawhide cord, and
boots with curled toes. A bruise swelled her left eye, and
her wrists were tied to her saddle horn.

"Hey," Sandy said, "isn't that—?"

"Shhh."

4

CUNO HUNKERED OVER his stew, as though interested only in eating, but he cut his eyes to the yard. The three riders reined up at the hitch rack, their sweated horses blowing, tack squeaking. Hearing them, the old man went to the door and stood there, gawking.

"What's to eat, old man?" one of the newcomers said.

The old man nervously wiped his hands on his apron as he stared at the girl sitting her horse before the hitch rack, her slanted eyes hard, her face expressionless.

"I said what's to eat, old man?" the newcomer said again. He took a folding knife from his pocket and cut the girl's wrists from her saddle horn.

"I got stew and soda biscuits. Stew's a dime. Coffee's a nickel extra."

"Sounds good to me. Sound good to you, Bob?"

"Sounds good to me," Bob said as he tied his horse at the rack. "But then, it'd sound good to me if it was that stinky soup the Injuns make out of buffalo guts."

"We haven't ate since last night," the first rider said. "We're hollow as gourds." He grabbed the girl's arm and pulled. She tumbled out of the saddle and hit the ground with an angry wail and a string of curses tart enough to wilt a cactus. He smiled down at her, then slapped her face with the back of his hand.

The girl tumbled sideways in the dust and fell silent.

Inside the roadhouse, Sandy gave Cuno a meaningful look. Cuno glanced at him. Shaking his head, he returned his eyes to his stew.

"Lucky, is that any way to treat a lady?" Bob asked his partner from the stoop. He and the old man were staring down at the girl, who'd climbed back to her hands and knees. She'd frozen there, trying to get her senses back.

"There ain't no lady here, Bob," Lucky said. He was a big man, as big as Cuno, with a thin blond beard over a sun-scorched face. He wore a yellow neckerchief and bull-hide chaps, a Colt hanging low on his left thigh. "Ain't no lady ever used the language this little bitch has used on us."

"Who is she, anyway?" the old man asked.

Lucky shrugged. "Didn't catch her name. We bought her off an Injun trader."

The girl turned to the old man. "They nabbed me off the trail!" she yelled. "They beat and raped me and tied me to my horse."

"Ah, bullshit," Bob growled. He was big, but several inches shorter than Lucky. He wore a gray-red beard on his doughy face, and his big, pale belly protruded over his cartridge belt, splitting his greasy shirt open at his belly button. "We paid good money for the little bitch, and we're gonna get our money's worth."

Lucky turned to the old man. "After lunch, we're gonna enjoy ourselves, if you get my drift. If you don't have a room, we'll use your barn. Me and Bob are so randy we've been seein' women instead of water mirages since Durango."

The old man hesitated, regarded the girl warily. "Yeah, I have a room. . . ."

"How much?"

"One dollar for the day."

"We'll take it," Bob said. "Lucky, bring the girl inside."

"We gonna give her something to eat?" Lucky asked.

"Nah," Bob said, ducking his head as he crossed the threshold into the roadhouse. He grinned. "We'll give her something to eat later."

Cuno lowered his head again, and swabbed his bowl with a biscuit. Out of the corner of his eye, he saw the man named Bob move into the room and look around. Presently, Lucky pushed the girl through the door and followed her in.

"Get over there and sit down on the floor where we can keep an eye on ye," Lucky growled, giving her another shove.

She stumbled across the room and into the far wall. She jutted her chin at the two men again, snapping her eyes, the left one bruised the color of an evening sky. "I told you sumbitches to leave me be, or I'll—"

She stopped mid-sentence, her eyes widening as Lucky raked his Colt from his holster and fired. The bullet brushed the girl's hair as it plunked into the wall over her right shoulder. She whipped her head at the splintered hole in the wood. She turned her horrified gaze back to Lucky, then slumped down to the floor, crossing her arms over her chest. Staring at the floor with defeat, she said nothing more.

So far, she hadn't seen Cuno and Sandy sitting at the long table only a few yards away. Cuno was glad she hadn't. He didn't want her to recognize them until he was ready.

"Now, then," Lucky said, holstering his pistol and turning to the old man, "where's our chow?"

The old man stared at the girl, fingering his curly beard nervously. "Comin' right up," he said, shuffling toward the kitchen.

Bob and Lucky took a seat at the other end of the long table from Cuno and Sandy. They didn't say anything, just sat down, removed their filthy hats, and grumbled a few sentences to each other. Their food came quickly, and they dug in like trail hands.

Sandy flicked his eyes at Cuno several times. He was having trouble finishing his stew. He knew trouble was coming. He just wasn't sure when. No way Cuno was going to stand by and let a girl be assaulted . . . even if she had tried to kill him.

The girl kept her eyes on the floor, the very picture of dejection. From her angle, and because of the shadows, it would have been hard for her to see Cuno and Sandy clearly, even if she had raised her eyes.

Cuno lingered over his coffee, staring across the table toward the kitchen door, behind which the old man had busied himself washing dishes. After Bob and Lucky had sat down, Cuno didn't look at them once.

"Well," Cuno said finally. Sandy held his breath. "That sure was good." Cuno donned his hat, dug in his pocket for some coins, which he tossed on the table, and climbed to his feet with a sigh. "What say we powder some trail, boy?"

Sandy just looked up at him, eyes wide with wary expectation.

"Why don't you bring our horses out front? Unhitch the girl's from the rack, too."

Sandy's heart shuddered. He stood slowly, not looking at Lucky and Bob. He heard them both stop eating.

"Say what?" Bob said.

Cuno was still looking at Sandy. "Run along."

Sandy turned and hurried out the door. He stopped there, several feet from the threshold, and turned to see inside the cabin's smoky, shadowy interior.

The girl had lifted her head and was gazing at Cuno now, wide-eyed. "Massey?"

"Get up and go outside. The boy's bringing your horse."

Lucky stood up suddenly, straddling the bench and turning to Cuno, an indignant expression on his face. "Hey, what in the hell you think you're doin', boy?"

"I'll be takin' the girl off your hands," Cuno said mildly. His right hand hung down near his .45 Colt. "You should thank me. I'm doing you a favor."

Bob stood slowly, regarding Cuno warily. "What's she to you?"

"She tried to kill me last night. It's kind of a blood bond we have."

"You aim to kill her?" Bob asked.

"No, much as I'd like to."

The two waddies regarded him sharply, turning him over in their heads. What were they thinking? Finally, Lucky frowned and took one slow step back. "Hey, wait a minute, Bob. The girl called him Massey."

"So?"

"He's Cuno Massey. I seen his face on a wanted poster in Farmington."

Bob frowned, his gaze cemented to Cuno. "You that gunslick with the bounty on his head?"

"I know what you're thinking," Cuno warned, reading their dull minds. "You think you might be able to pick up some easy cash, maybe winter down in Arizona. Forget it."

Bob and Lucky stared at him hard, their chests rising and falling.

"I'll just be taking the girl and riding out of here." Cuno's eyes shuttled to the girl. He jerked his head, indicating the door. "Go on out, Marlene."

Dumbfounded, Marlene rose slowly.

Bob threw his arm out. "Hold it right there, girl. You ain't goin' nowhere." To Cuno, he said, "She's ours. Like we told the old boy, we bought her from Injun traders."

Cuno's voice was low and even. "No, you didn't."

"You callin' us liars?" Bob asked.

"Hold it, Bob," Lucky said. "This young bastard's killed a lot of men. They say he's fast and cold-blooded."

"He don't look cold-blooded."

"Well, that's what they say."

Bob studied Cuno with renewed interest, cocking his head to one side and slitting his eyes. He winced and chewed his lower lip. "He don't look so tough to me. Lucky, do you realize that if we took this shavetail down and collected that five thousand, we wouldn't have to brush-pop beef for pennies and piss water for a good, long time?"

"I realize that. But I also realize we can't collect the five thousand if we're pushin' up sod."

Cuno smiled tightly. "I don't think Lucky's feeling so lucky, Bob. Maybe you better listen to him."

"Yeah, you better listen to him," the girl said. She'd lowered herself back down to her butt and was watching the proceedings with interest. "Massey shot my whole gang last night—bang, bang, bang, and they were all wolf bait. Buried in flies even as I speak."

"You mean you didn't bury your pals, Marlene?" Cuno chided.

"Nah," the girl said. "I had bigger fish to fry, like fig-urin' out where my next meal was coming from. Then I ran into these two needle-dicked blowflies."

"Needle-dicked, eh?" Bob growled through gritted teeth, his heavy cheeks flushing. "You'll pay for that later, you saucy little bitch."

"I don't think so, you fuckin' pervert."

Bob trembled with rage, his chest puffing and his fists clenching, but he managed to keep his florid gaze on Cuno. Lucky didn't look as angry; he looked worried about the possibility of swapping lead with Cuno.

"Go on outside," Cuno told her. "Don't worry about them. They're gentlemen."

Confidently, the girl rose. Neither Bob nor Lucky said anything. They stared at Cuno, Bob's wrath fairly dagger-ing from his deep-set eyes. The girl walked past both men, turning to them and making a crude gesture. Then she breezed past Cuno and out the door.

Cuno hadn't looked at her. He'd kept his eyes on the men. They stared back at him, Bob with barely contained rage, Lucky with cautious apprehension. Out of the corner of his eye, Cuno saw the roadhouse proprietor poking his head out the kitchen door, a worried look on his face.

"Now, I'm going to walk out that door, and if either of you so much as sneeze my way, I'm gonna drop you."

He'd begun backing toward the door before he'd even finished the sentence. Neither Bob nor Lucky said any-thing or made a grab for their side arms.

At the door Cuno paused, scrutinized the two men one

more time, then slid quickly to the side and descended the
stoop. Sandy was leading the two horses across the yard.
The girl stood by the hitch rack.

Accepting his reins from Sandy, Cuno said, "You two
mount up and ride north. I'll be right behind you."

Sandy and Marlene swung onto their mounts and headed
up the trail at a gallop, tearing up large gouts of sod and dust
behind them. Cuno mounted Renegade and jogged to the
edge of the yard while hipping around in his saddle to watch
the cabin's door. Bob appeared in the doorway, belly splitting his shirt open, looking mad.

"Don't trail us," Cuno warned. Then he reined Renegade
around and galloped after Sandy and Marlene, feeling dark.

Sometime he'd like to eat a meal and not have to back
out of the room afterward. He doubted that would happen
anytime soon. At least, not until he paid a visit to a man in
Julesburg . . .

When he'd caught up to Cuno and Marlene, he asked
her, "You gonna make it?" indicating the bruise around her
eye.

"Why wouldn't I?" she spit. "I s'pose you think I should
thank you for saving my hide back there." She shook her
head. "There wasn't no need. I was waitin' for my moment,
then those two were gonna be singing' soprano, if you get
my drift."

Sandy turned to Cuno. "What's she mean—'soprano'?"

Cuno opened his mouth, then closed it. He had to get
this boy back to civilization fast. "Never mind," Cuno said.

They rode for a while in silence. Cuno was listening,
casting cautious glances behind him.

"What's the matter?" the girl asked him at last.

"You two ride ahead. I'm gonna hole up here for a
minute."

Cuno reined his horse into a crease between two low,
grassy buttes. A dry creek bed threaded the crease, filled
with rocks and driftwood.

"What's the matter?" Sandy asked him.

"We're bein' shadowed."

"How do you know?" Marlene said, wrinkling her brows as she gazed back the way they'd come. "I don't see nothin'."

"He knows," Sandy told her grimly. "Come on."

Behind them, Cuno kneed Renegade several yards up the creek. When he'd passed behind a hill, he dismounted, shucked his Winchester, and jacked a load into the breech.

5

CUNO RAN BACK around the hill, climbed halfway to the top, and hunkered down behind two boulders grown up with weeds. He didn't have to wait long before the clomp of horse hooves grew in the south. Bob and Lucky appeared, trotting their horses, reins held high.

"I don't know about this, Bob," Lucky said with worry in his voice. "You sure we can take that kid?"

"For five thousand dollars," Bob grumbled, "I can take any kid. We just sneak around and ambush him."

When they were directly in front of Cuno, he got to his feet and squeezed his rifle. "What'd I tell you fools?"

The two riders sawed their reins back and whipped startled glances at the hill. With their free hands they grabbed for their pistols.

Neither one cleared leather before, crouching, Cuno squeezed off two quick shots, blowing both men off the backs of their skittering mounts. They tumbled, kicking up dust. Bob cried out as his horse kicked him, twisting, bucking, and galloping through a crease across the trail. Belly-down, Bob crawled toward his fallen gun, grunting. He didn't make it six inches before his face hit the dirt and his body fell still.

Cuno lowered his rifle to his waist and let gravity carry him down the hill at a controlled run, leaping rocks and sage tufts. He walked over to Lucky, who lay in the middle of the trail on his back, spread-eagled, groaning and sighing. Blood bubbled from his nostrils and mouth. His chest, too, was blood-matted where Cuno's slug had taken him through his left lung, nicking his heart.

Cuno shook his head and said with disgust, "I told you not to trail me."

Lucky only stared up at him through pain-wracked eyes, more blood bubbling from his lips. Feeling the old revulsion, the old fury at the man who'd put the bounty on his head and had made a battlefield of his life, Cuno lowered the rifle barrel to the drover's temple and fired.

His mouth a grim slash in his face, he set the Winchester's barrel on his shoulder and walked around the hill to his horse.

Ruben Pacheca reined his hammerheaded buckskin to a halt on the wooded hill, and tipped his head back, sniffing.

"Smells like coffee," he told his horse. Gazing around, blinking against the hot afternoon sun that angled over the cedar-wooded hills humping up around him, he looked for smoke or horses. He listened for voices—any sign of a camp—but neither saw nor heard anything.

"Well, I'll be," the bounty hunter said. "Must be comin' from those buttes up that way. Coffee, eh?" He shook his head as he kneed the buckskin down the hill, following a meandering game trail.

Pacheca had intended to put on trail supplies back in Alamosa. For obvious reasons, he hadn't been able to do so, and he was plumb out of coffee. He could do without sugar and salt and baking powder. Hell, he could do without flour if he'd laid in enough jerky or side-pork. He'd

found whiskey to be a hazard on the trail, causing him to
let his guard down and lose the trail he was following. Beer
didn't get him as drunk, but it plumb tasted like sow drool.

The one thing he could not do without for more than
two or three days was coffee.

At the bottom of the hill, he could no longer smell the
belly wash. He might've been imagining it, but didn't think
so. A vagrant wind current had brought the smell to his
nose, and if there was one thing his nose knew, that thing
was coffee.

Someone was brewing coffee in them buttes one divide
to the northwest. . . . Damn, he'd love to have a cup of
that brew.

He followed a brushy freshet through a fold in the hills,
climbed a low ridge, and reined to a stop. Twitching his
nose, he smelled the coffee again, and his tongue tingled
with anticipation. His eyes brightened as he regarded the
dugout in the ravine below, through which a creek glistened in the sunlight, trickling over rocks.

The dugout looked like the opening of a mine shaft,
knocked together with unskinned logs and a Z-framed
plank door decorated with elk antlers. Another, larger door
was on the right to allow for saddle stock in the right side
of the shelter. The place was a line shack used by winter
range riders, mostly in emergencies when blizzards broiled
over the San Juans, catching the riders several miles from
the main compound.

Pacheca remembered the place. He'd camped here before when tracking men in this country. On his previous
visits, the place had been abandoned. Men were obviously
in the area now, however. No horses were present, but
smoke curled from the tin stovepipe, tinging the air with
the unmistakable smell of cedar smoke and coffee.

Pacheca's mouth watered. Half-smiling to himself, he
gigged the buckskin down the slope, splashed across the
creek that rose to his horse's knees, then urged the mount
up the opposite bank to the cabin facing out from the
eroded, adobe-colored ridge.

He dismounted, slipknotted the reins to the hitch rack. The buckskin lowered its head to drink from the stock trough, half-filled with oil-colored water in which hay and corn hulls floated.

"Anyone home?" Pacheca hailed the cabin.

When no one answered, his hand found the doorknob and turned. He pushed the heavy door open—a door built to withstand attack from Indians and grizzlies—and ducked his head to peer inside.

He recognized the three sets of bunks on which blankets lay rumpled, the table built from split logs, the trapdoor under which emergency food stores were cached. The place smelled like man-sweat, wood smoke, and coffee. On the sheet-iron stove in the back rear corner gurgled a black percolator scorched by many fires.

Pacheca stretched a grin, lumbered his bulk inside, grabbed a tin mug off the table, heedless of the dried grounds inside, and filled the cup to the brim with the thick brew, black as death and issuing tendrils of gray, scorched-smelling steam.

"Just how I like it."

The giant lumbered back to the table and sat down. He produced his briar pipe from a pocket, packed it, lit up, and sat enjoying the pipe and the coffee. He was on his second cup and second pipe when the buckskin sent up an alarmed whinny.

Pacheca gave a sour grunt. He'd enjoyed the peace and quiet and his pipe and coffee, and wasn't ready to have it compromised by others. If he had his druthers, there would be no other people on the planet. Just him and his horse, a cabin up in the Shining Mountains stocked with salted beef, buffalo tongue, and countless bags of Arbuckle's. Maybe a fat Indian wife . . .

Standing, he loosened his sawed-off Winchester in its holster. Cup in hand, he made the door in two long, thundering strides, and threw it open. He crouched through and stood just outside the threshold, his eyes narrowing as a string of six riders appeared along the creek. A stout dray

trailed them, driven by a seventh man and pulled by a pair
of mules. The dray was mounded with limbed tree trunks
secured with chains.

Pacheca stood scowling as the riders and dray turned
from the creek and climbed the sloping bank, heading for
the cabin. The riders rode slouched in their saddles, as
though tired from a hard day's work. They were all dressed
in ordinary trail garb—dusty hats, neckerchiefs, calico or
buckskin shirts, and chaps. When their gazes found Pacheca
and the buckskin, their heads came up, necks stiffening a
bit with cautious curiosity.

They came on at their same, plodding pace, the wagon
trailing. The leader, a short, burly man in a sugar-loaf sombrero, eyed the bounty hunter skeptically, said something
over his shoulder. The man behind him replied. They both
went back to staring, keeping their hands near the guns
holstered on their hips.

"Who do we have here?" growled the leader, canting his
head to one side, giving Pacheca the twice-over.

"No reason to get iron-horny, boys," Pacheca said as
the riders approached. "I'm just enjoyin' a cup of your
joe. Thought I'd spend the night." He squinted at the sun
falling behind the western hills. "Be dark soon. No point in
movin' on till mornin'." He sipped his coffee and smiled,
savoring the taste before letting it go down with an audible
whoosh.

"I didn't ride back here and put the coffee on just so's
some grub-liner could drain the pot," said the thin redhead
in a black hat, curling his pink lips back from his teeth.

Pacheca's head did not move, but his gaze flicked to the
man, studied him with a slight narrowing of his colorless
eyes. The man held his gaze for a time. Then, as if of their
own accord, his eyes ran up and down the giant frame.
Awed by the size and ugliness of the stranger, the redhead
twitched and blinked, deferred to the short, burly man who
was apparently the crew's foreman.

The foreman had been appraising the giant, too. Appro-

priately impressed by Pacheca's size and grizzled countenance, he allowed a fateful sigh to whistle through his
chapped lips. He gave his head a single shake. "Well, hell,
I reckon there's enough food and coffee for one more."

The giant had already turned and was heading inside the
cabin. Doing so, he noticed one of the men eyeing him nar-
rowly. He turned to the man now—a medium-tall hombre
with a pitted face, shaggy sideburns, and a small, flat-tipped
nose, as though a file had worked on it. Judging from his
dark complexion, he had some Mexican blood. He gazed at
Pacheca with open menace in his small eyes. At Pacheca's
glance, the man looked away, turned his horse with the others, and headed for the rope corral on a flat section of creek
bank, his chaps flapping around his legs.

Pacheca stood in the doorway, staring after the riders,
his eyes at once hard but with thoughtful curiosity crinkling the corners. He'd seen the man before. The man had
recognized the bounty hunter. That much was obvious. But
where had the two crossed paths . . . ?

Then it came to him. A slow smile stretched the bounty
hunter's lips, deepening the lines in his eye corners. He
nodded as though at his own private joke, then sipped his
coffee and went inside for a warm-up.

A few minutes later, the cowboys filed in, slapping dust
from their chaps and hats. Pacheca watched them from the
table, where he sat sipping a fresh cup of coffee without
saying anything. He didn't like the company, but there was
nothing he could do about it. The waddies were preparing
the shack for the winter, bringing in wood. They'd probably brought canned food from the main compound and
stashed it under the floor.

Sensing the big man's animosity, as well as the strange-
ness common to loners, the men didn't say anything to
him, either. They talked amongst themselves, but with a
self-consciousness due to the giant stranger's presence.

With a nod to trail civilities, they offered him some of
the mule deer they fried, but he told them he was fine with

the coffee and his own hardtack and jerky, which he'd produced from his saddlebags when he'd unleathered his horse and corralled it with the others.

He sat at the small table while the others ate around him, only one braving his stench enough to join him. Throughout the evening, Pacheca was aware of one pair of eyes boring a hole through him. The bounty man didn't react to it. Instead, he sat at the table, drinking one cup of coffee after another, nibbling his jerky, a look of barely contained amusement bunching the half-bleached beard and deepening the red of the birthmark bleeding up from his cheek to his forehead.

"Care for a game of cards, mister?" one of the men finally asked him, when everyone had finished eating and the dishes had been washed and returned to the cabinet. A fresh pot of coffee gurgled, the cork was popped on a whiskey bottle, and the cigarette smoke thickened as it webbed along the ceiling, drifting slowly through the half-open door.

The drover, a short man with glittery eyes the color of rifle bluing, riffled the cards as he pulled up a chair across from the giant, regarding the man expectantly.

Pacheca shook his head. "Don't gamble," he grumbled, and sipped his coffee.

"Well, in that case," the steely-eyed cowboy said, raising his eyebrows and glancing meaningfully at the table, "you, uh, mind . . . ?"

Pacheca looked at him, looked at the table, slowly realizing as he saw several other men skulking up from the bunks that they wanted the table for a poker game. They wanted him to move.

6

PACHECA LOOKED AT the cautious, expectant faces around him, his eyes squinting, as though he were thinking it over. Finally, he shrugged, slid his creaking chair out, and climbed to his feet, having to duck his head under the rafters. He poured fresh coffee at the stove. Adjusting the sawed-off Winchester on his hip, he turned to one of the bunks, glancing at the man boring a hole through his back with his eyes.

The man reclined on a lower bunk near the stove. He lay on his back, muscular arms crossed over his chest. Black, wiry hair shone through his sweaty, denim shirt unbuttoned to his belly. He wore a big Smith & Wesson .44. His hair was long and thin, hanging well over his ears; his shaggy sideburns were flecked with gray.

"Hi there, Pete," Pacheca said with an affable nod, lowering his beastly frame to the bunk upon which he'd already piled his gear.

The man stared at him, his dark eyes flickering slightly. No expression came to his face.

"You two know each other?" the short foreman asked.

When the other man didn't say anything, Pacheca

shaped a wry smile as the leather ties creaked and groaned beneath his bulk.

"Me and Pete? Hell, yeah. I brought him to Judge Parker—what was it, Pete—six years ago?"

The man didn't say anything for a moment, just burrowed his dark gaze into Pacheca. Then, quietly: "Seven. I was in for six. Got out last year."

The four men sitting at the table tensed. They turned to look at Pacheca, then shuttled their curious, cautious glances to Pete Cervantes.

Cervantes's face was impassive. He was still staring daggers into Pacheca. The bounty hunter smiled back at him, his legs hanging over the bunk and crossed at the ankles.

Cervantes said without inflection, "He clubbed me over the head in Port Early. Laid me out cold. I was just standin' there drinkin' a beer."

"Oh, boy," one of the other men whispered darkly.

Pacheca's self-satisfied smile remained. It gave an even more carnivorous look to his ugly face. "Sometimes it's easy."

"Yeah, easy," Cervantes said. "Only, I didn't do what they said I did."

There was a long, fragile silence. Smoke curled above the table, where the four cardplayers sat frozen, regarding Pacheca and Cervantes worriedly. Another cowboy sat on the floor near the door, reclining against his saddle. He'd been reading a magazine, which now lay facedown in his lap. The other man had been stoking the stove against the gathering chill. He now stood by the stove, a split log in one hand, a branding iron he'd used as a poker in the other, a penny cigar smoldering in his chipped, protruding teeth. Like the others, he shuttled his gaze between the bounty hunter and Cervantes, his face tightening, as though bracing himself for a fight.

The foreman, who sat at the table, quirley drooping from his lips, was the first to break the silence. "What'd they say ye did, Pete?"

Cervantes swallowed, his prominent Adam's apple

bobbing in his leathery neck. "Said I kidnapped a girl from a schoolyard, raped her, cut her throat, and threw her body down a privy." He shook his head slowly. "Only, I didn't do it. Those gringos just said I did 'cause I was the only Mex in town that day. Put a five-hundred-dollar reward on my head. Lucky I got a God-fearin' judge, or they woulda hanged me."

Pacheca chuckled. "That five hundred came in handy, too. Winter was comin' on, and I needed a new horse and saddle."

Cervantes's eyes darkened, as though an opaque, inner lid closed over them. His raw features remained impassive. "They found the man who really did it. The town's harness maker confessed on his deathbed. That's why they quit me breaking rock at the federal pen."

The room was so quiet that the horses were heard stomping in the rope corral, blowing and chomping hay.

"Oh, boy," someone let slip through his teeth on a sigh.

The foreman removed the cigarette from his mouth and regarded Cervantes with hard authority. "I don't want no trouble in here, Pete. You and the big man have somethin' to settle, settle it outside."

Cervantes stared at Pacheca, his eyes two agates in his dark, impassive face. He almost looked bored. His tin coffee cup lost in his bearlike paws, Pacheca stared back at him, his own eyes glittering like river rocks—amused, waiting.

Finally, Cervantes raised a hand from his chest in a casual gesture of supplication, his hard gaze still holding Pacheca's. "I have nothing to settle. Ruben was just tryin' to earn a living, right?"

The silence stretched as taut as before, released finally by the foreman, who sighed audibly. "That's more like it," he grumbled, turning to the redhead beside him. "Frankie, deal the cards."

The redhead shuffled and dealt, the other players sweeping the cards up in their hands. As the mood in the cabin lightened, the players teased each other, elbowing, hooting, muttering playful curses.

The man who'd been stoking the fire lay on his bunk, reading. The man on the floor took up his own magazine and smoked as he flipped the pages.

For a time, Pete Cervantes's hard eyes remained on Pacheca, whose own gaze held firm, bright with smoldering, vaguely taunting amusement. Finally, Cervantes turned onto his side, fluffed his pillow, bent his knees, and sighed. In a few minutes, he was snoring.

Pacheca sipped his coffee and smoked another pipe. Idly, he said to the room in general, his low, thundering growl rising above the low din, "Anybody see a kid named Cuno Massey hereabouts?"

Pacheca hadn't said much. That's why the sudden inquiry stopped the card game outright, all heads turning to the bounty hunter spilling over his bunk.

"Massey?" said a sandy-haired youngster at the table, his voice thick from whiskey. He cut his rheumy, hazel eyes to the foreman. "Ain't that the gunslinger wanted up north, Walt?"

Frowning thoughtfully, Walt nodded as he stared at Pacheca through cigarette smoke twisting up from his lips. "Heard about him in Del Norte. Someone seen him in the country a few days back."

The redhead turned to the foreman, his gray eyes sharp. "You don't s'pose that was him camped along the Prairie Dog?"

Pacheca turned his ugly face to the kid. "Medium-tall, blond, wide-shouldered? Has a shavetail boy with him."

Pacheca had seen Massey when he'd passed through Phoenix several weeks ago, only he hadn't known the kid was wanted until he'd seen the dodger hanging in the sheriff's office in Alamosa. The young man's hard eyes and authoritative bearing had made him memorable. He'd looked like he'd be handy with a hogleg, only he didn't swagger, which was odd for someone his age. Pacheca was always on the watch for possible bounties, and the cool caution in Massey's eyes had bounty written all over it.

"Reckon that fits," the redhead said reluctantly. "Had a sprout with him."

Pacheca's gaze sharpened, his nose twitching. "When'd you see him?" he asked.

The redhead's eyes flicked to the bounty hunter's. Indecisively, as though he wasn't sure he should answer the question, he glanced at the foreman again, who only stared at him expectantly, awaiting an answer himself.

The kid shrugged, his face pinched and insolent. "Two, three days ago."

"Two, three days ago, huh?" Pacheca mused aloud.

"That's what I said, didn't I?"

"Which way was he headed?"

"How the hell should I know? When I seen him, him and the sprout were rubbin' down their horses." The redhead gave a caustic snort and glanced around the room at the other cowboys, as though looking for backing in his mockery of the stinky stranger. "How should I know which way he was headed?"

The foreman chewed his quirley, regarding the bounty hunter pensively. "How much he have on his head, this Massey?"

"None of your damn business," Pacheca growled, relaxing against his saddle, a wickedly satisfied light in his eyes. He was on the right trail. Like Pacheca had figured, Massey was headed north. North didn't figure, because he was wanted up north, but north was indeed the direction he appeared to be heading. Which meant Pacheca was heading that way, too.

"I heard five thousand," the redheaded kid snapped out, casting a defiant glance at Pacheca.

"Five thousand dollars?" the man reading in his bunk said, frowning over his book. "For what?"

"I heard he wiped out half a town during a holdup," the redhead said. He formed a gun with his right hand. "Pow! Pow! Pow! Just like that. Laid out the schoolteacher and the preacher and the sheriff and two deputies—deader'n a hangman's soul."

Cervantes had stopped snoring. He turned to the kid, pinching his face together angrily. "Butte, will you shut the hell up? Can't you see I'm tryin' to sleep?"

The kid scowled at him, wrinkling his nose. He dropped his eyes sheepishly, picked up his cards. "Walt asked me. . . ."

"Now, where were we?" the foreman asked, picking up his cards and scrutinizing his hand.

"Five thousand dollars," said the sandy-haired youngster, whistling and shaking his head.

In a few minutes, Cervantes was snoring again. While the four men played poker, the two others read.

Pacheca smoked his pipe, tapped the dottle onto the floor, rose, and ambled outside. He peed off the porch, returned to the cabin, removed his tunic and boots, and lay back down on his bunk, head against his saddle, hat pulled low across his eyes.

In spite of all the coffee he'd drunk, he was able to ignore the whoops, occasional curses, and table whackings rising from the card game, and quickly fell asleep. He'd be up early, riding north.

He wasn't sure how much later it was when he opened his eyes. The room was dark. Snores sawed up from the bunks around him. The fire showed a dull red around the door of the sheet-iron stove.

In his sleep, the bounty hunter had heard something that had set off an alarm in his unconscious mind. Instinctively, he did not turn his head, only rolled his eyes around to regard the dark-hazy room, his ears so alert that he heard the muffled hoot of a distant owl and the breeze scuttling under the eaves.

A board squeaked.

Suddenly, a figure darted to his right, blocking out the fire glowing around the stove doors. Light glinted off a knife blade. Pacheca's right hand flicked upward, closed around a wrist about six inches from his neck.

A grunt sounded as the bounty hunter squeezed the hairy wrist in his massive paw. As the bones in the wrist ground together audibly, Pacheca closed his left hand around the hand holding the knife.

One hand on the attacker's wrist, the other on the attacker's knife hand, Pacheca squeezed the man's knuckles together around the handle. The knuckles popped and cracked like tinder. The attacker howled and cried, punched Pacheca twice with the other fist—flailing, glancing blows—then stopped and used that hand to try and pry his right hand free of the bounty hunter's devastating grip.

An amused half smile pinching his bearded face, Pacheca twisted the knife blade away from him. Pointing it at Cervantes's belly, grinding the man's wrist and knuckles to a literal pulp between his fingers, he applied even pressure.

Cervantes did a bizarre, stumbling dance as he tried to fight the knife away from him. But his strength was no match for the bounty hunter's.

Screaming and panting against the building, grinding pain, against the flashing blade's twisting progress toward his belly laid bare between the flaps of his open shirt, Cervantes flailed at the bounty man's unrelenting grip and his gradual, unstoppable thrust.

"*Eeeeee-yiiii!*" he cried as the blade tip poked his hairy belly.

The sharp blade plunged through the skin easily. Blood gushed, darkening the blade. Bunching his lips, Pacheca heaved. The blade disappeared into Cervantes's gut, releasing blood and viscera like wine from a flask.

Cervantes screamed again, dropping his chin to his chest, sobbing, panting as the fluid gushed out of him. Pacheca released the man's ruined right hand. Cervantes dropped to his knees and fell on his side, holding the knife blade now with his left hand, his right flopping uselessly on the floor.

Only about half a minute had elapsed since Pacheca had awakened, and the others were just now milling, calling out feebly, bewildered and frantic. Cursing, someone struck a match. There was the squawk of a lantern door. The lamp was lit, its wan glow revealing Cervantes on the floor before Pacheca's bunk, shivering and gasping like a landed fish. The thick dark blood rushed out of him, the pool expanding around his curled body.

Several unintelligible inquiries were grunted before someone yelled, *"What the goddamn hell is goin' on?"*

Several of the men, clad in only long underwear, were up and shuttling wide-eyed, open-mouthed stares between the dying Cervantes and Pacheca, who sat with one foot on the floor, ducking his head under the upper bunk. He heard the unmistakable sound of a revolver being shucked from a holster. As the bounty hunter pushed himself up from his bunk, he grabbed his sawed-off Winchester.

Before he could bring it up, his stocking foot slipped in Cervantes's blood, and he fell to a knee. Steadying himself with one hand on the bloody floor, he raised the Winchester just as the redheaded kid, his hair sleep-mussed, raised a Colt from across the table upon which cards and tin cups were still strewn.

"No, Butte!" the foreman yelled as he struggled to free his own six-shooter from the holster hanging from a chair back.

"That murderin' bastard!" the kid screamed, thumbing back his Colt's hammer.

Still on one knee, Pacheca steadied the Winchester in both hands, jacked a shell, and fired an instant after the redhead's bullet buzzed past the bounty hunter's ear and thumped into the wall behind him. Pacheca's slug took the kid through the throat, throwing him back against the door with a booming thump that made the lantern flicker.

The others were yelling now, storming about the room, grabbing frantically for firearms. Calmly, with a dexterity surprising for a man his size, Pacheca went to work with the Winchester, jacking and firing, jacking and firing. The rifle leapt in his hands as he slid it from left to right, the shells flickering in the lantern light, arcing over his shoulder and rattling to the floor behind him.

The wails of the dying men could be heard between the Winchester's intermittent explosions. Through the burst of powder smoke, Pacheca watched the grisly death dances performed before him, the half-clad men tumbling onto bunks and against the walls, careening off the wood stove and timber posts, blood splashing, lips stretched back from teeth in pain-wracked snarls and grimaces.

A body flew into the table, which broke with a booming crunch. The windows were shattered by ricochets. Dying, someone broke the lantern, casting the room in smoky darkness.

When the hammer ticked against his firing pin, empty, Pacheca lifted his head and gazed through the smoke haze. No shadows moved in the darkness. The silence lay heavy, broken only by a few grunting death spasms and clipped sobs. The foreman, sitting up against the wall in the cabin's front right corner, gave a liquid sigh and jerked a leg as though wanting to stand.

Pacheca stood with a grunt, lowering the Winchester to his side. Fumbling around in the dark, he found the lantern, got it lit. Looking around, he saw that the only man still breathing was the foreman sitting against the front wall, wide-eyed with shock.

No use wasting another bullet. Pacheca grabbed his nine-inch bowie from his belt sheath, grabbed a fistful of the foreman's hair, and ran the blade cleanly across the stubbled neck. The foreman gurgled, eyes snapping. Pacheca let his head drop over the blood bibbing his chest.

Pacheca straightened and looked around the room again. He sighed, scratched his head, hacked phlegm from his throat, and spit. Turning, he peered out the broken front window. It was a clear night. The constellations told him it was only about two, three in the morning.

He was on the stalking trail, damn it all. He needed his sleep.

The bounty hunter scratched his head again, and stooped to rub his bloody right hand on the shoulder of a dead man's underwear top. He uncorked a canteen, took a long drink, then stalked back to his bunk. Avoiding Cervantes's blood pool, he collapsed into the bunk, drew up

the blanket, rolled over, closed his eyes, and heaved a rest-
ful sigh.

In two minutes, his bearlike snores rose to the blood-
splattered rafters.

7

CUNO WAS LEADING Sandy and Marlene
east through a steep-walled valley when a din rose on the
breeze. He sawed back on his reins and lifted his chin, his
sharp green eyes sweeping the landscape.

The noise seemed to be coming from ahead and left, beyond the canyon's north ridge. Sooty smoke lifted in that
direction—a gauzy, gray column rising straight up in the
cloudless sky.

"Lay back," he told Sandy.

He gigged Renegade into a lope for fifty yards, then
turned off the valley floor and up the sage-tufted ridge. The
paint's racing hooves thudded heavily, digging at the sandy
soil. Near the top, Cuno halted the horse, slipped out of the
saddle, and shucked his Winchester.

"Stay, boy," he ordered, dropping the reins and running
in a crouch toward the hilltop.

Before he got to the hill's brow, he doffed his hat and
dropped to his knees. Crawling awkwardly, the Winchester
in his right hand, he made the brow of the hill and peered
over the ridge.

His face bleached. His stomach tightened. He turned

back to where Sandy and the girl sat their mounts at the base of the hill and made a slashing motion with his left hand, meaning, "Stay out of sight and for God's sake keep quiet."

He edged a slow, careful gaze into the valley where a cabin and barn sat, burning, flames leaping from the walls and roofs—two thundering infernos sending thick puffs of sooty black smoke skyward. Two copper-skinned Indians loosed arrows into the paddock stock while several more killed pigs in the pen adjacent to the barn, the animals' squeals raising the hair on the back of Cuno's neck.

Gritting his teeth and squeezing his rifle stock with anger, Cuno forced himself to stay put. There was nothing he could do to help the poor settlers.

One of them, a man, lay by a stock trough near the barn, an arrow through his neck. Blood glistened from the scalped crown of his head. A woman lay in a flower patch near the porch, her dress bunched around her ankles, her legs spread wide, blood glistening from her cut throat.

Another female—a girl in her teens—lay near the corral. Her naked body sprouted arrows from her breasts and belly.

Shuttling his gaze toward a stand of trees surrounding a glimmering creek on the other side of the farmyard, Cuno saw another, smaller figure lying prone, facedown in the bluestem that all but hid him. The boy had apparently been cut down while fleeing toward the creek. Several arrows jutted from his back and legs. The very top of his scalp, too, was gone.

One of the bronzed, war-painted Kiowa was holding the rope reins of three spotted ponies at the far edge of the yard. He yelled toward the paddock, where another painted savage shot arrows into a prone horse. The stout, old plow-puller scissored its hooves, lifted its head, and screamed above the roar of the burning buildings as the arrows pierced its ribs.

The horse's piteous screams raked Cuno's spine. He raised his Winchester to his shoulder, leveling a bead on the Kiowa torturing the horse. It was an idiotic move that could very well get him killed, but his hands worked of their own accord, leveling the rifle's barrel on the Kiowa's chest.

He let out a breath, and his finger took up its slack. The Kiowa had just pulled another arrow from his quiver and was notching it to the bow when the bullet ripped through his chest, spinning him around and sending him sprawling, bow and arrow flying.

Cuno drew the rifle back, quickly ejected the smoking shell, levered a fresh round into the breech. He snugged the butt up to his cheek, squinted down the barrel.

The brave holding the horses was jerking his head around, looking for the shooter. Yelling, he turned to two others running from the pigpen, their hair flying about ochre-streaked faces, quivers slapping on their backs.

Cuno planted the bead on the horse-holder's chest, and fired. Confident he'd hit his mark, he recocked and turned to the others.

One of the pig-killers ran crouching toward a stock tank while the other hightailed it to the horses. Loose now, the herd was skittering and sidestepping, wide-eyed, ready to bolt.

The brave heading for the stock tank, a woman's dress flapping bizarrely about his legs, was almost there. He lowered his head for a dive when Cuno's bullet pinked him. The brave screamed and dropped, clutching his right leg.

Meanwhile, the other brave had mounted a pinto. The horse bucked and kicked. The brave jerked on the reins, got the horse headed toward the ridge on which Cuno was lying, and heeled him frantically into a low, rocking gallop.

The horse planted its ears back against its head as it stormed across the cinder-shrouded yard. It crossed a dry-bed creek and mounted the hill, avoiding the horse trail and heading straight up toward Cuno.

Cuno rose onto his knees, sighted down the barrel. He fired, missed, recocked, fired, missed again.

He cursed, slammed another bullet home, fired again. The bullet grazed the Indian's ear. The brave whipped his head angrily, wincing, driving his heels even harder into the pinto's ribs.

The pony came on, head and ears down, mane whipping, nostrils blowing. The brave crouched behind the horse's head. Cuno saw little but his blowing black hair and a silver pendant flapping off a shoulder.

To stop the Indian's frantic ascent, he'd have to stop the horse.

Reluctantly, he levered a shell into the Winchester's breech and planted a bead on the pinto's broad, star-blazed chest.

From Cuno's left, a gun popped. The Indian cried and pitched to his right side, jerking on the reins. In a wink, horse and rider were sprawling, rolling in the grass, kicking up a thin yellow dust cloud. The horse quickly climbed back to its feet, shook its head. Blowing, it looked around in shock, wondering what had happened.

Cuno was wondering the same as he watched the brave roll several yards down the hill and pile up against a lichen-flecked boulder and lay still, leaving a swath of bent, crimson-flecked weeds in his wake.

The horse turned, trotted a ways along the hill, stopped, looked around again cautiously, then lowered its head to graze.

Cuno turned to his left. Marlene Stratton stood atop a flat-topped boulder, holding her Spencer rifle in her hands, smoke wisping from the barrel. Her uncombed blond hair whipped out behind her in the breeze. Her shabby felt hat shaded the upper half of her face, but her lips stretched a sardonic grin.

She turned the grin on Cuno. "You don't think I miss all my shots, do you?"

Cuno chuffed. "Surprised you didn't backshoot him."

He looked around for the boy. Sandy was standing at the base of the hill, holding the reins of their three horses in the shade of a large, cracked rock, gazing uphill expectantly. Cuno raised his rifle, signaling all was well, then turned and walked down the farm side of the hill.

He paused by the dead Indian brave hugging the boulder. Kicking the brave over, he saw the blood-smeared face and bloody right side, where Marlene had pinked him. The brave's eyes were closed, an odd death-grin shaping his lips.

"Stay here with the boy," Cuno told Marlene, then jogged down the hill, using the occasional sage clumps and cedars to break his descent.

Casting his gaze across the yard, he saw that the brave he'd plugged by the stock tank was gone. Cautiously, he approached the tank. The seed-flecked dirt was scuffed and blood-streaked. A furrow, made when the man had dragged himself off, traced an arc around the burning barn.

Cuno followed it, holding the Winchester high and ready, a fresh shell in the chamber.

He'd walked out past the trash heap and a dilapidated work wagon, when a savage scream cut the air. Cuno wheeled to his left, lowering the Winchester. The Indian exploded up from a weedy swale—a hideous visage in a young woman's torn gingham dress, with bits of antelope hide wrapped in his oiled braids. A knife blade sun-flashed in his raised right hand.

Leveling the rifle on the Indian's belly, Cuno fired. At the same time, the Indian swatted the rifle sideways. The bullet sailed wide, tearing into the wagon with a sharp crack.

Cuno dropped the rifle and grabbed the Indian's knife-wielding fist just before the blade could tear into his face. He jabbed at the Indian's chin with his left fist. The Indian was moving too quickly and forcefully, twisting and bobbing, and Cuno's jab only grazed his shoulder.

The Indian was all muscle and sinew. Cuno felt the man's coiled, compact strength. The muscles writhed like snakes beneath the sleeve of the girl's dress, which stopped short at the brave's copper forearm.

The brave's eyes found Cuno's. They were deep brown and white-ringed, the pupils expanding and contracting with the man's frenzy. Suddenly, his eyes slitted and his face wrinkled as he ripped the hand from Cuno's grip with an animal-like howl, then slashed with the knife.

Cuno ducked, pivoted, punched the Indian's jaw with his right fist, this time landing it solid.

The Indian staggered. Cuno stepped into him, punched him twice in the belly. The brave staggered several more steps, grunting and yelling in Kiowa, dragging his wounded right leg.

Cuno was about to finish him with a roundhouse. The brave regained his balance, set his feet, and swung the knife low across Cuno's belly, slicing his buckskin shirt two inches up from his belly button.

Cuno pivoted, did a shoulder roll beyond the slashing knife, and came up with another roundhouse, landing it squarely on the back of the brave's head. As the brave stumbled forward, Cuno grabbed the brave's arm, swung around, dropped to a knee, and cracked the arm across his thigh.

It was a savage blow. Cuno heard the elbow pop and the bone crack, felt the arm give, watched it bend unnaturally back upon itself, splitting the dress sleeve.

The Indian dropped the knife, fell, and threw his head back, howling.

Cuno straightened, unholstered his Colt, aimed at the brave's broad, pain-twisted face, and fired. He'd aimed for the Indian's forehead, but the Indian had been thrashing too wildly for an accurate shot. Instead, the round, dark hole appeared just below his left eye.

Both eyes widened. The jaws clamped shut. The brave threw his head back, blinked twice, and relaxed, expiring with a long sigh and a fart. A blood bead appeared at the bullet hole, slowly trickled down the Kiowas's cheek, glistening crimson in the afternoon sun.

Hearing hoofbeats, Cuno turned. Marlene and Sandy were tracing a broad arc around the burning cabin, squinting against the hot wind whipped up by the flames.

"I thought I told you to stay on the ridge," Cuno said to Marlene.

"How long were we supposed to stay there—a couple weeks?"

Cuno frowned. The girl's insolence was annoying. He was getting shed of her as soon as they got to a settlement.

"Get back up there and signal me if you see any Kiowa headed this way. From the tracks I saw in the yard, there were plenty more than these four. They might have heard our shooting."

The girl looked around at the burning buildings, the two bodies she could see from this angle. "Don't make much sense to me, you stirrin' up more trouble. I mean, looks like all the white folks were already dead."

"Do as I say, will you?"

The girl gave a caustic snort, turned her horse around, and galloped up the ridge.

Cuno turned to Sandy. "Help me dig a hole, boy."

It was late in the afternoon when one large hole had been dug near the creek. Cuno and Sandy dragged the bodies out from the yard and arranged them gently in the hole. Cuno mumbled a few words he remembered from church. Hollow words. He didn't believe in such words anymore. There was a point when words just didn't make sense anymore, and he'd gone beyond that point a good time ago.

He leaned on the shovel and stared at the arrow-riddled bodies lined up side by side in the hole. The blankets he'd found covered only part of them. The women were still naked. The man's head was a black mass of dried blood, his scalp no doubt decorating a Kiowa's lance.

The digging, the death, made Cuno think of July.

For a few seconds, he watched her running across a sun-lit field in his imagination, with Indian paintbrush and bluebonnets in her fist, her dark hair flying, her free hand holding her straw hat on her head. Her full lips stretched a playful grin as she skipped past him, looking back at him, smiling lovingly, then disappearing in an aspen grove.

In Cuno's mind, she reappeared, lying at the bottom of the grave he'd dug for her back on their farm where they'd planned to raise a family—stock the cabin with bawling brats, as Cuno had joked. It hadn't turned out that way. They'd been married less than a year. At the bottom of the deep, dark hole in his memory, the blanket he'd wrapped her in was blood-crusted and already stiffening with the death it enshrouded.

He forced the image from his mind. Turning away from the dead family at the bottom of the fresh hole, he looked at the cabin, burned to the ground and still smoldering. Blood clung to the grass, marking the path by which he and Sandy had dragged the bodies from the yard.

Cuno turned to the boy, staring wanly into the grave, his round felt hat clutched to his chest. "Let's get it done, boy, and get the hell out of here."

8

SANDY AND CUNO quickly filled in the grave, and arranged rocks over it to hold the carrion at bay. Cuno wished he could have erected a marker, but nothing indicated the family's identity. Maybe a neighbor would erect one later.

As the sun angled low behind the mountains, Cuno, Sandy, and Marlene left the smoldering buildings behind. They rode across a high, slanting mesa, the peach light of the setting sun bathing the sage tufts and rabbit brush, the rocky ridges above them pitting with shadows.

They followed a game trail down the other side of the mesa and found a good camping spot in a canyon rimmed with tamaracks and cedars. They unsaddled their horses by the flickering light of their cook fire, the coffeepot chugging softly above the queries of the first night birds.

Nearby, a wide stream gurgled over stones. After Cuno had eaten some jerky and drunk some coffee, he grabbed his war bag, walked to the stream, knelt down, and doffed his hat. The Kiowa's knife slash was painful and needed cleaning.

To that end, he shrugged out of his buckskin shirt and examined his belly in the starlight reflecting off the water. He couldn't see much from this angle—his head shaded his gut—but he didn't think it looked as bad as it felt.

Weeds crunched behind him. He jerked around quickly, slapping his Colt's butt.

"Hold on, hold on," Marlene Stratton said in her characteristically dry fashion, moving toward him. "It's just me. After all the shootin' I've seen you do, I've decided I can live without that bounty on your head."

"Five thousand dollars would take a girl a long way."

Ignoring the remark, she knelt beside him. "Let me see."

"It's just a little cut. I can take care of it."

"Let me see," she demanded.

"Kind of pushy, aren't you?"

"Move your hands and sit back so I can see something besides your hat."

He did as she bid, and she lowered her head over his belly, inspecting the wound in the flickering starlight. She probed with her fingers.

"Ouch!"

"It's more than just a little cut," she carped. "It's a half-inch deep. It needs a good cleaning and wrapping."

"I can do it myself."

"I've never known a man yet who can clean a wound proper. Now just wait here and don't move around. I'm gonna grab some bandage cloth from my saddlebags."

When she returned, he was smoking a cigarette, gazing at the dark line of rimrocks across the gurgling stream, under a velvet sky strewn with diamond chips. Far away, a coyote bayed; another answered.

As Marlene knelt beside him, unwrapping a spool of white cloth, he regarded her curiously—this pretty little outlaw girl with a waiflike face and the demeanor of a wolverine.

She set the cloth aside, dampened her rag in the stream, and began cleaning the wound again. He was surprised by the gentleness of her hands, carefully dabbing at the crusted blood, instinctively knowing how much pressure would do.

She dipped the rag, dabbed at the far left edge of the ragged gash, lowering her head to see better in the starlight. She turned to him suddenly.

"Stop lookin' at me."

"Sorry. You're prettier than I figured."

Saying nothing, she wrung the rag out in the stream. Turning back to him, she removed the quirley from his lips, took a drag, sucking the smoke deep into her lungs, and exhaled. Returning the cigarette, she dabbed again at the cut.

He sat back on his hands, smoking while she worked, trying to ignore the caress of her fingers, the soothing tickle of her long hair wisping against his chest while she bathed the wound, occasionally brushing a shoulder. He could hear her breathe, felt the warmth of her body close to his.

He was trying to distract himself from her by concentrating on the coyotes that had set up a distant yammering, when she stopped, took the cigarette again, and drew on it. She stared at him, their faces only a foot apart, her eyes cool and frank, holding his gaze without expression. Exhaling, she gave him back the quirley.

"It's as clean as I can get it. Now I'll wrap it."

She'd tied several cloths together to make one long one. She wrapped it tightly around his waist, securing it over the gash, her hair brushing his shoulders, her chest rising and falling behind the shirt she'd tied closed with rawhide strips. Her pert breasts pushed at the fabric of her plaid flannel shirt as she worked, and he couldn't help envisioning how they'd appeared when he'd tackled her in the meadow.

Small and firm, impossibly smooth, pink-nippled and creamy.

He sighed and looked away, feeling guilty, ashamed. July had been dead less than a year, and here he was, staring at some outlaw girl's breasts.

"Would you like a better look?"

He looked at her sharply. She'd knotted the bandage

and was sitting back on her heels, staring at him, hands on her thighs.

"No," he said, feeling his face warm.

She placed her hand on his thigh, freezing him. Her hand through his jeans was warm, almost hot. It inched slowly toward his stiffening member. She set her hand on it gently, with no pressure at all, and sat staring at him, her face sober below the brim of her man's felt hat.

"I won't beat around the bush, Cuno Massey. You strike a right manly figure, and I'd be your girl if you wanted. That said, I won't hold you to no hand-holdin' or longtime courtin' if you want to sleep with me tonight."

He opened his mouth to speak, but his voice caught in his throat. Before he could try again, she said, "I know you lost your wife. I've never been in love before, so I'm not an authority on the subject. All I know is she isn't here. She's never gonna be here again. But you and me—we're here."

While she spoke, her fingers had been working at the rawhide thongs on her shirt. Now she slipped the shirt off her shoulders, let it fall, doffed her hat, and lifted the undershirt over her head.

Cuno watched silently, his heart thudding dully, his body warm. Her hair rose with the undershirt, and fell about her naked shoulders. She replaced her hat on her head, staring at him and grinning.

She took his right hand, moved it to her breast, held it there with both hands, the nipple stiffening beneath his palm. "Does this make up your mind for you?"

He jerked his hand away. She frowned. He felt his heart race, his chest heaving, his passion building, making him dizzy. It had been a long time since he'd been with a woman.

His thoughts, his reluctance, evaporated. He grabbed Marlene's arm, drew her to him, kissing her, pressing his mouth hard against hers, feeling the warm, petal-like softness of her lips.

She seemed alarmed at first, almost frightened by his sudden intensity, her body rigid. She turned herself over, melting into his arms, curling her legs, snuggling into him as he kissed her, opening her lips for him. He pressed his mouth to hers, enjoying the feel of her warm, slender body engulfed in his, the sweet taste of her probing tongue.

Finally, he pushed her away, held her there with his big hands on her rib cage, gently taking one firm breast in his mouth.

She gasped, shivering, arching her back and digging her fingers into his shoulders. He licked one nipple till it jutted, hard as a thimble, then worked on the other as she shuddered and softly moaned, running her hands hungrily across his shoulders, down his back, digging in the fingernails enough to begin hurting.

All passion and heedless, hot wanting, he turned her over, helped her out of her jeans, then struggled out of his own clothes. She helped with the gun belt. He turned to her, ran his hands down her long, slender body, pale and shadow-relieved in the starlight. He only vaguely heard the stream's tinkling as he mounted her, breath rasping with his passion, unable to control himself any longer, unable to wait.

When he was situated between her legs, she locked her ankles around his back, ran her hands down his arms as he worked atop her, grunting and sighing and pumping with his need.

He let go with a long groan, every muscle in his body tensing. She gasped and sobbed, her soft body clinging to his, trembling. After a while, he lifted up on his arms, rolled away, started to stand.

"Where are you going?" she asked.

"Wait here."

He slipped quickly into his jeans, socks, and boots. Donning his gun belt and hat, he strode quietly back to the camp, where the fire sank low in the stone ring.

The boy was asleep on his back, head against his saddle, blanket drawn up. His mouth slack, chin lifted, Sandy snored softly, his breath catching in his throat.

Quietly, Cuno grabbed his and the girl's blankets, and

walked back to the stream. The indentation they'd made in the grass was vacant. She was in the water. He could see her shadow, hear her splashing around, see the water reflecting the sky's glitter.

He dropped the blanket, set his hat and gun belt down, slipped out of his boots and jeans. Naked, he stepped into the stream, feeling the icy chill numb his feet and inch up his legs.

After a few steps, he lowered himself into the water, instantly soothed and refreshed. He walked to where she lay in the shallows on her back, her wet hair slicked back against her head, legs and feet floating. She threw her head back, her chest rising, revealing her small, round breasts above the sliding water, jeweled with shining droplets.

"Take me again," she said. "Take me here."

He knelt beside her, lifted her in his arms with both hands, kissing her long and deep, flattening his tongue against hers. She moaned deep in her chest, and then he was sliding her gently toward shallow water across the stream, where the bottom was soft and sandy. He laid her down, spread her legs, mounted her, controlling his passion, expressing it more gently this time.

After a few minutes, she wiggled out from under him, pushed him aside. He rolled onto his back as she quickly straddled him, her face pinched with desperate concentration. Then she was rocking atop him, bouncing, her wet hair dancing about her shoulders, his hands caressing her breasts, stroking her slender hips.

Later, hand in hand, they returned to the shore, and he gently dried her with a blanket. When she'd dressed, he told her to return to the fire, where she'd be safest.

"Where are you going?" she asked as he dressed.

"I'm gonna keep watch atop that butte yonder. I don't want any surprises tonight."

He turned to walk away. She grabbed him harshly, threw herself into his arms, and kissed him, mashing her lips passionately against his. Swallowing, breathing deeply, she drew away, staring into his eyes.

"Don't worry," she whispered. "No ties. I just enjoyed tonight, that's all."

"I did, too," Cuno said with a smile. "Thank you. I needed that more than I needed anything just now."

She dropped her chin, lifted it, lips forming a shy smile.

"Good night," he said, turning away and starting for a stone ford in the stream.

"Good night," Marlene said behind him, watching him skip rock to rock on the balls of his feet.

When he made the shore on the other side, he walked through shrubs and looked around, squinting into the darkness. Finding a vague path, he started up the butte, stepping between sage clumps, tufts of rabbit brush, and greasewood.

He slipped between two boulders and made the gravelly crest, breathing hard, still thinking of Marlene writhing beneath him.

It was hard to get her out of his head. What sweet forgetfulness their lovemaking had been. Underneath was a lingering guilt.

It had been a long time since he'd known such release. For a long while, he'd lost himself in her body. He'd forgotten all the blood and carnage, the face of his dead wife, the faces of all the men he'd killed, the violent jump and bark of his Colt as yet another man went down for the last time.

He hunkered down on his haunches and peered down the hill columned with the black trunks of pines. A small creature scuttled across the pine needles several yards ahead and to his right. Probably a raccoon.

Beyond the tree tops, he could make out several dark hill folds that shone dully in the starlight, the ridges lumpy with rocks. To the west were the steep slopes of the San Juans blotting out the sky. In the east were the plains.

If trouble came, it would no doubt come from the plains. He'd spend the night here, dozing and keeping watch. It was quiet up here. He'd hear horses and riders long before they approached the camp.

He walked up and down the ridge, looking around,

stopping to listen, then found a small hollow of rocks, hunkered down, pulled his hat low, and closed his eyes. He'd sleep a while, wake in an hour, and take another look around.

He hadn't dozed fifteen minutes before he heard gravel crunch beneath a boot. Startled, he snapped his eyes open.

A dark figure in an enormous, tasseled sombrero stood over him. The slender silhouette of a rifle jutted from under the man's arm, slanted at Cuno's head, the bore yawning wide.

The line of the man's mouth stretched a dark smile. *"Hola, amigo."*

9

CUNO SENSED A bullet coming.

An eye blink after he'd reached up and swatted the rifle's barrel with the back of his hand, the gun barked. The flash was blinding. Unable to see his attacker, he lashed out with his right foot, connecting solidly with the man's soft crotch.

The man groaned.

Still seeing the red of the rifle's flash, Cuno bolted up and forward in an arching dive. He flew into the man, burying his head in the attacker's belly, throwing him backward. The two hit the ground hard, and the man punched Cuno's jaw, rolling him on over his head and sideways.

Blinking his eyes clear, his jaw pounding, Cuno checked his slide down the slope, looked up, and saw the man climb heavily to his feet, clutching his groin with one hand, reaching for the revolver on his hip with the other.

Cuno grabbed his own gun and fired.

"Dios!" the man cried, firing wide, stumbling backward, and dropping to his knees. Dark liquid oozed through the fingers clutching his right breast. *"Ay, caramba!"*

He stuck out a hand, eased himself down, grunting and groaning with the pain, cursing in Spanish.

Cuno walked several steps toward him, stopped, leveled his .45 on him. "Who are you?"

The man puffed his cheeks out, lifted his head. He was a small man, probably no taller than five-six or -seven. Mexican features with a slender mustache curled on the ends. He wore a short, embroidered jacket and tight trousers with two rows of hammered metal discs down both legs.

He stretched a ragged smile, his eyes hooded from pain and shock.

"Marlene," he said through a sigh, stretching his lips back from small, yellow teeth. "Marlene Stratton." The smile disappeared for a moment, reappeared again.

Then the man's eyes grew heavy, and his head dropped sideways. The hand holding his chest fell, but he was still breathing.

"What about her?" Cuno said, feeling a frown dig into his brow. He moved forward, knelt over the man, jerked his shoulder. "What about Marlene?"

The man's throat fluttered, but no reply came to his lips. He was out.

Cuno cursed and looked around. The night was silent. Nothing moved down the slope amidst the trees. If the man had been with someone, his partner or partners would no doubt have revealed themselves by now.

But what about a horse?

Cuno holstered his revolver and retrieved the Mexican's guns—a .38 revolver and a heavy Sharps .56—which he chucked away in the darkness, hearing it clatter against rocks. Holding his revolver down low at his side, he walked down the slope, stepping sideways and grabbing tree trunks to keep his balance. When he'd walked a ways, he turned into a shallow ravine traversing the hill diagonally, stopped, and whistled softly.

He listened. Hearing nothing but a distant cougar scream, he whistled again.

From straight up the brushy ravine rose a horse's snort, a

soft, inquiring whinny. Cuno moved ahead through the brush. Gradually, a horse's silhouette appeared before him—a fine-boned Arabian with a saddle liberally trimmed with silver.

"Easy, boy, easy," Cuno said perfunctorily, figuring the horse probably understood only Spanish commands.

He eased up to the horse tethered to the branch of a deadfall tree, patted the horse's forequarter as he sidled up to the animal and rummaged through the saddlebags.

He was looking for a clue to the gunman's identity. All he found was a spare pepperbox pistol, cooking utensils, knives wrapped in oiled rags, a few sacks of dry goods, jerky, and tobacco, a letter written in Spanish, and a folded piece of paper. Unfolding the paper, he saw that it was a reward dodger bearing his own sketched likeness and a reward amount: five thousand dollars. Dead or alive.

Nothing in the bags revealed the Mexican's identity, but that didn't matter now that Cuno knew what he'd been after.

How did the man know Marlene?

Cuno heard himself sigh, tired and puzzled, as he untied the horse's reins from the branch and began leading the Arabian back the way he'd come. When he saw the man lying on the slope above him, he slowed and unholstered his revolver, then continued leading the horse up through the trees.

As Cuno approached and dropped the reins, the man didn't move. His labored breathing rose in the quiet night, and his legs jerked with pain spasms. Cuno bent over him, grabbed his arm, and pulled him easily over his shoulder, then heaved him over his saddle, belly-down, head hanging over the far side of the horse. The Arabian reared and skitter-stepped, smelling blood.

"Easy, easy," Cuno soothed.

The horse had calmed, but kept twisting looks at its comatose rider draped over its saddle. Cuno led the mount over the brow of the hill and down toward the creek murmuring through the cottonwoods, dappled with shimmering blue pools of starlight. He and the horse splashed across the rocky ford and entered the camp in the trees.

"It's Cuno," he announced as the two figures jerked upward in their blanket rolls. "Sandy, throw a log on the fire."

The girl's voice was sleep-gravelly, incredulous. "What are you doing . . . where'd you get the horse? Who's that?" she asked.

"Had me one of those surprises I was worried about."

Cuno tied the horse to a tree and pulled the Mexican off his saddle, gentling him to the ground near the fire. Sandy stirred the glowing embers and added several small branches, which smoked, then ignited, small flames leaping. When Sandy added a driftwood knot, the fire grew even brighter, finding the pain-wracked, mustachioed face of the Mexican bounty hunter. He was still alive, eyes fluttering, his left hand finding the wound on his chest.

Cuno figured he'd lunged him. He probably wouldn't live long.

Cuno looked gravely at Marlene, who sat up in her bedroll, hair hanging in her face, her features drawn from sleep. "You recognize this son of a bitch?" Cuno asked her.

She scowled at the faint accusation in his voice. "Why should I?"

"He mentioned your name."

Her eyes rose to Cuno's. A frown riding her blond brows, she stood and, clutching the blanket around her shoulders, stepped around the fire and stood gazing down at the wounded Mexican.

"Pablo Mirado," she said. "Mexican gunslick. He rode with my pa . . . until he killed him." She stared down at the Mexican blandly.

"This man killed your father?"

Marlene nodded. "Someone was bound to, sooner or later."

"Why?"

"Pa was a cardsharp when he wasn't robbing miners down in Mexico. He tried fleecing Mirado in Tucson, and Pablo ventilated him."

"You don't look all that broken up about it."

Marlene looked at Cuno, her slanted eyes cool. Her

voice was characteristically ironic. "My pa was a snake who mixed with snakes. Sooner or later he was gonna get bit."

She returned her sharp gaze to the Mexican. "So Pablo came for you, too, eh?" She shook her head and turned a wry half smile on Cuno. "You're a dangerous fella to be ridin' with."

Cuno was about to respond when the Mexican grunted several Spanish words, snapping his eyes. Cuno retrieved his saddle and propped it beneath the Mexican's head.

Kneeling beside the man, he said, "What are you saying?"

The Mexican snapped his eyes again until they found the girl staring down at him. The same smile he'd smiled before appeared on his face.

"Well . . . Marlene . . ." He tried to say more, but coughing wracked him, and he passed out again, his head falling back against the saddle.

Cuno glanced up at the girl. A troubled look clouded her face, and she quickly turned away, sat back down on her blanket roll. "He's out of his head," she said. "Probably saw us together on the trail. Probably figured after he killed you, he'd kill me, too, or worse. Filthy bastard."

She avoided Cuno's curious stare as she pulled some jerky from her saddlebag and chewed a piece off.

Cuno turned to Sandy. "Gather some more wood, will you, boy? I'm gonna wash this blood off my hands in the stream, and fill a coffeepot."

He grabbed the pot and headed for the stream. He was halfway there, when a gun blasted behind him. Dropping the pot, he palmed his gun, wheeled, and ran back toward the fire, his heart pounding.

The fire's circular glow revealed the girl standing near her bedroll, the rifle in her arms aimed at the Mexican. She'd blown out the man's chest. He looked flattened, as though dropped from the sky, his left cheek pressed snug against the saddle. His eyes were open, his mouth drawn wide as though fighting for air.

"I turned my back on him," Marlene said flatly. "When I turned around, he was lunging for Sandy's pistol."

Cuno heard running footsteps to his right. Sandy appeared between two bushes with an armful of branches, his face flushed, his eyes wide with surprise. "What happened?" the boy asked.

Cuno walked over to the Mexican, shuttled his gaze to Sandy's big Remington protruding from the holster coiled near the boy's blanket roll ten feet away.

"Kind of a long way for him to lunge in his condition, wasn't it?" he asked Marlene.

She lowered the rifle, set it against a tree, and shrugged. "What was I s'posed to do? He was going for a gun. Where I come from, you don't pussyfoot around the man who killed your pa. Even if your pa was a snake."

She sat down again, knees up, and pouted into the fire as she nibbled her jerky.

Cuno cursed, grabbed the dead man's boots and dragged him into the brush, then retrieved the coffeepot, which he filled in the stream after washing the man's blood off his hands and arms.

When he returned to the camp, Marlene and the boy were stretched out in their bedrolls, Marlene lying on her side, blanket pulled up, rifle propped nearby. Seemingly unfazed by the night's excitement, she slept soundly, breathing deeply, the fire coating her cheek with warm, copper light.

Sandy only dozed, his breath shallow, bullet-crowned hat tipped over his eyes, arms crossed on his chest.

The fire snapped and burned down, the pine resin sizzling in a green log. Beyond the camp, the night grew very quiet. Not even a coyote yammered in the far distance. A light breeze tussled the tops of the cottonwoods, softly rustling.

Cuno studied the girl as she slept. She'd been lying about the man going for Sandy's gun. Maybe she'd shot the man for revenge.

Or could there have been another reason?

10

RUBEN PACHECA SCRAMBLED up the grassy slope, stumbling and grabbing at the tough brown brush, occasionally falling to a knee. As clumsy as he was, he moved with unusual speed for a man his size.

Holding his long-barreled Henry rifle with one hand, the other holding the cut-down Winchester snug against his thigh, he came to a game trail rising vertically across the slope. He rested on the flat trail strewn with deer pellets big as .56-caliber slugs, hands on his thighs as he heaved air into his lungs.

Damn wind was always the first to go. He should have stayed in the mountains and worked his traplines. That's how a man stayed fit, how a man stayed young. Riding horses, trailing men, was how you lost your youth.

But no mountain man ever earned five thousand dollars for one pelt, Pacheca thought, a slight, humorous flush showing beneath the bleach-bearded side of his face.

Hearing muffled thuds on the slope above, he glanced up the hill in time to see four mule deer—a small buck, two does, and a yearling—spring-hop toward a low thicket near the brow, then disappear down the hill's other side.

Pacheca scowled, his eyes hooding.

Damn. He hoped the three men trailing him didn't see the fleeing deer. They might suspect the game had been spooked from this side. Any tracker worth his salt would suspect as much. But then, good trackers wouldn't have let the sky outline them for as long as those three had when he'd spotted them atop a tabletop mesa twenty minutes ago.

Pacheca scrubbed a grimy sleeve across his soggy brow and, instead of following the more gently climbing game trail, bolted straight up the slope. He dug his stovepipe boots into the flinty soil, tugged at a chokecherry branch, broke it, and fell.

Undiscouraged, he rose again, took several more huffing, puffing steps, fell to a knee once more. Again, he heaved himself to his feet, trudging higher.

Ten feet beneath the ridge, he dropped to both knees, doffed his wide-brimmed hat, and crawled to the mountain's brow. His lungs heaved, felt like they'd been raked raw with sandpaper. His shirt under his arms and down his back was soaked with sweat. Hacking penny-tasting phlegm, he inched up onto the narrow, scree-covered ridge until he could see down the other side.

Three riders moved along the slope, riding from Pacheca's right to his left, on a course that would place them straight below him in a few minutes. Three men in dusty trail garb, carbines in their saddle sheaths. On their shirts and vests, badges winked in the sunlight.

They rode single file. The first and second riders were hipped around in their saddles, watching the deer hightailing it down the ridge behind them. The third man tipped his head low, cupping a match to a cigarette.

The sons of bitches had sniffed out his trail awfully fast.

The bounty hunter grumbled a curse, chewed his lower lip. He wasn't sorry he'd killed the lawmen. Regret wasn't in his makeup. Besides, they'd deserved the head-lopping. These three badge-toters were just another boil on Pacheca's ass, a distraction from his quest for Cuno Massey and the five thousand dollars on his head, which Pacheca intended to haul up to Julesburg in a burlap sack.

Muttering curses, Pacheca lifted the Henry, jacked a shell in the breech, and stared down the barrel. The first and second men were looking for trail sign, heads lowered so all he could see were their hat crowns.

The third man—a redhead with bushy side whiskers and a battered slouch hat riding a blue roan—was smoking his quirley and jawing at the others loudly enough for Pacheca to nearly make out the words. None appeared concerned about the deer. Despite the fact they'd sniffed out his trail, their carelessness marked them as tinhorns. Tinhorns trying to make a name for themselves by taking down the best man-tracker this side of the Mississippi and south of the Yellowstone.

Pacheca snorted and shook his head with disgust. He didn't have time for these slips. He snugged his cheek against the rifle butt and had almost laid a bead on the first rider when the second man drew back on his reins, halting his buckskin.

Pacheca lifted his head and stared over the top of his gun. What was he up to?

The second rider said something to the others, then dismounted, rummaged around in a saddlebag, and came up with field glasses.

"Uh," Pacheca grunted. "Ain't as dumb as I thought."

The man's mouth moved beneath a thin, black mustache. He turned to the hill and raised the glasses, began sweeping the ridge from northwest to southeast. The others had drawn up and were regarding him curiously, occasionally running a glance along the hilltop to Pacheca's right.

Allowing himself a grin, Pacheca snugged his cheek against the Henry's worn stock, set the backsight inside the foresight on the blue-and-black-checked shirt of the man with the field glasses. Slowly, he lifted the bead to the man's head, waiting as the man moved the glasses toward him.

Suddenly, the man's slow pivoting motion stopped. He

held the glasses steady, staring straight up at Pacheca. The left lens flashed silver in the sunlight.

The bounty hunter snickered through a grin, his eyes hooding as he laughed. He held his breath, took up his finger slack. As the man, frozen, opened his mouth to speak, the gun barked and jumped. The bullet was on its way, slicing the high, thin air, making a slight tinkling sound as it smashed through the right lens of the field glasses, burrowed through the casing, plunged into the lawman's eye and continued through his brain plate and out the back of his head.

Pacheca lifted his cheek from the gun butt, stared down the slope.

The man had stumbled back against his horse, dropping the shattered glasses. The horse was rearing and skittering sideways, its ass smeared with its rider's blood and brains. The horse plunged straight down the hill, the man tumbling after it, rolling. His companions were looking up the hill, wide-eyed with shock and confusion, checking down their own crow-hopping horses.

Even from this far away, Pacheca could see their fear-blanched faces, the whites of their terrified eyes.

The bounty hunter climbed to his feet, raised the rifle, and fired three quick shots, kicking up sod and pebbles at the feet of the lawmen's jittery mounts. "Go on home!" Pacheca yelled. "Go on home to your mommas before I take ye over my knee and slap the livin' shit out of ye!"

He fired three more rounds from down low at his side, jumping and yelling like a hobgoblin. The bullets kicked up more dust and sod as the lawmen, spying no near cover, reined their horses down the hill. They hunkered low over their saddle horns as their mounts raced for a rocky, cone-shaped knoll.

Pacheca stretched his arms out, tipping his head back and yelling, spittle flying from his lips, "Go home, ye badge-totin' tadpoles. Be gone with yous. Boo!" He threw his head back even farther, his guffaws echoing like summer thunder around the valley below. *"Or you'll goddamn wish you had!"*

With that, he turned and started back down the hill, cursing and laughing under his breath.

When he came to his horse tethered in a hollow at the bottom of the hill, he slid his Henry into its boot and mounted up. As he started off, heading straight north along the first front of the San Juans, he glanced skyward. There was enough light left for another hour's riding, he figured.

He rode for a half hour, following several intersecting creeks through brushy, broken flats along the base of the foothills. He checked his back trail often, finding no sign that he was being followed, which meant he probably wasn't. Like most good man-trackers, Pacheca knew when his own trail was being dusted.

The shavetails had no doubt thrown their dead partner over his horse and headed back to wherever they'd come from, riding soft on the shit in their pants. Remembering the fear in their faces as they watched their partner's head explode like a pumpkin all over his horse's ass, he was sure of it.

Boys like that—cow waddies turned tin stars—might talk a good game. But one well-placed .44 slug was all it took to fill their shorts with goo.

Near sundown he spotted a brown blur slip between two rocks on a low ridge to his left. He tied his horse to a cottonwood, shucked his Henry, and walked up a cut near the base of the hill, returning twenty minutes later with a medium-sized mountain lion draped over his shoulders, its dun coat burnished by the setting sun.

That night he roasted a quarter of the lion on a rough wooden spit over his campfire, drinking the coffee he'd stolen from the line shack. He watched the cat's juices drip over the rocks and sizzle amongst the coals, his eyes bright with expectation. He salivated like a dog.

There was nothing like the taste of fresh-killed painter. Any mountain man would tell you that. Nothing like the faintly musky smell mixing with that of the coffee, delivering an otherworldly aroma to the giant's expanding and contracting nostrils.

Nothing like it in the world.

Pacheca was on the trail early the next day, as he always was, heading north, hoping he'd run into Massey, or hear of him in one of the settlements. Late afternoon found him riding his big buckskin along the south fork of Comanche Creek, pondering stopping for some coffee, when he heard a sound like a child's laughter.

He reined the buckskin to a halt and looked around, wondering if he was approaching an Indian camp. Seeing nothing but cedars and aspens on his left and the wide, shallow stream flashing as it trickled over stones on his right, he rode a few more feet.

The noise rose again, high-pitched and hard to identify but sounding human. It came from around a bend in the creek, on the other side of a low, brushy ridge upstream.

Fingering the butt of his cut-down Winchester, he reined the horse into the stream, splashed across, and reined up on the opposite shore. Dismounting, he led the horse into a notch in the hills, where several cedars stood twisted together in the heavy brush.

When he'd tied the horse to a branch, he shucked his Henry and walked around the base of the hill. Finding a fold, he turned right and, hearing more voices now—those of adults as well as children—climbed the hill on his left.

At the top, he crouched down and gazed through a V-notched boulder, into the valley beneath the hill. The stream split the valley down the middle, shining like a million pennies as the late afternoon sun rolled toward the high western peaks. On the stream's other side, five wagons were parked—a motley collection of platform-spring drays, a dead-axle dray, and a simple farm wagon with a seedbed and thick sides over which canvas had been stretched.

The mules had been picketed in a long line right of the

wagons and back against the trees. Nearer the river, six or seven youngsters roughoused, laughing as they tackled each other and ran splashing through the shallows. Bearded men in shabby felt hats milled, smoking pipes and talking near the rear of the farm wagon while the women—three, by Pacheca's count—were busy building cook fires and carving meat from an antelope carcass spread across a makeshift table, back legs forming a V.

As Pacheca watched the milling emigrants, the corners of his lips turned down with disappointment. The women were mostly broad-hipped gray-hairs dressed in gingham and calico. They walked like some men Pacheca had known. Once freed from their corsets, their breasts probably sagged to their belly buttons, and their thighs were no doubt as wide as whiskey barrels, their ankles stout as crock jugs.

No, wait a minute.

The giant's heart quickened. His eyes hooded as they shifted right of the main camp.

A girl appeared, stepping out of the woods, swinging a basket mounded with berries—mountain currants, no doubt. With long strides, her long, chestnut hair bouncing down her back in enticing swirls, she made for the cook fires, swinging the basket and smiling.

Sixteen, seventeen years old, Pacheca thought. A well-endowed girl, her bosom swelling out the simple, homespun dress. Full-hipped but long-limbed, slender, square-shouldered. A clean, open face with large eyes and a bold, self-assured demeanor—a real handful under the blankets, no doubt, but probably still a virgin.

With a warm twitch in his groin, the giant imagined what the girl would look like naked, the starlight glinting off her smooth, creamy skin and pert, saucy breasts with their petal-pink nipples.

He hadn't had a woman in a long time—not since he'd passed through Phoenix three weeks ago. He was as ripe as September chokecherry, his skin virtually splitting with the timeless carnal need.

In the encampment along the river, the girl proudly displayed the basket to one of the women, then set the basket on a tailgate and began helping the woman erect a spit over one of the fire rings. Pacheca watched the girl as he mulled a plan, thoughtfully tapping the Henry's barrel.

Finally, when a course of action had shaped itself, his eyes narrowed, and the giant retreated from the hilltop and returned to his horse. He splashed back across the river, traced a path through the trees, and made a wide circle around the emigrants' encampment.

Finding a small vale about seventy yards on the other side of the wagons but downwind from the mules, he unsaddled the buckskin and set up camp. Over a fire he cooked another quarter of the mountain lion and ate with relish, his hunger heightened by fantasies of the emigrant girl. He washed the tough but savory meat down with liberal portions of coffee.

When he'd finished eating, the sun was an hour down and the valley was shrouded in darkness. The breeze had cooled, and Pacheca donned an extra wool sweater under his bearskin tunic. He built up the fire, so he'd see it upon his return from the emigrants' camp, and lit out through the woods, stepping quietly through the silent forest, smelling roasting antelope mixed with the tangy scent of pine needles on the breeze.

It wasn't the smells that made his heart thump, his breath grow shallow, and the tip of his broad tongue dab at his bearded lips. It was the expectation, the images of the girl dancing just behind his eyes.

When he came to the edge of the trees, a good ways right of the mules, he saw the flickering fires and silhouetted figures moving about the encampment. The men were greasing wheel hubs and inspecting axles, while the women cleaned up after supper. Apparently, the younger children were already in bed, for Pacheca neither saw nor heard them.

It didn't take him long to find the girl he'd seen earlier, bent over a wreck pan warming on the fire, washing iron skillets and trenchers, her face shaded, her chestnut hair glistening in the firelight.

Pacheca waited a long time, watching the encampment, observing the girl as she went about her chores.

Finally, one of the women spoke to her. The girl nodded, stretched near one of the fires, so that Pacheca could imagine the dress drawn tight across her breasts. She kissed the woman's cheek, made up her bed beneath one of the wagons, then slipped away from the encampment, holding her skirts above the ground as she skipped across the rocks and into the trees several yards to Pacheca's left.

The giant bounty hunter's heart leapt. He couldn't believe his good fortune. He'd figured he'd have to wait until all the pilgrims were in bed, then steal the girl out from under the wagon at gunpoint.

Wheeling left, he made his way slowly through the trees, careful not to snap any branches. He'd walked several yards before he heard a slight hissing sound, stopped, and smiled.

His tongue darted over his lip, snakelike, as he moved even more slowly, more quietly, positioning himself between the hissing sound and the edge of the trees.

He stopped.

The hissing ceased, replaced by the sibilant sounds of underclothes moving along shapely calves and thighs, rising to enshroud a taut young ass. Pacheca swallowed, felt his face heat like a steam iron as the girl's skirts fluttered down over her legs.

The night was so quiet, the sounds from the encampment so muffled, that Pacheca heard the girl's regular breaths as she buttoned the dress.

Her shadow turned, started toward him. Crouching behind a tree, Pacheca waited. When she'd passed the tree, he straightened and reached out, crooking his huge arm around her neck, clamping his bearlike paw around her mouth, stifling her scream.

She tensed with shock and fear, kicked at his legs, lashed out with her arms. Unfazed by her resistance, his hand firmly in place, the giant leaned down and whispered in her ear.

"Do as I say," he rasped, "or I'll hack your whole family into bits small enough to feed a kitten!"

She froze, trembling, her eyes wide, her breath hot and moist against the bounty hunter's palm.

"Do you understand?" he whispered, blowing his fetid breath.

A tear trickled down the girl's cheek. Her face, nearly covered by the bounty hunter's huge hand, crumpled with fear. A muffled sob died in her throat.

At last, she nodded weakly.

His hand still over her mouth, Pacheca wheeled and half-dragged, half-carried her back toward his camp.

11

WHEN YOU'D BEEN hunted as long as Cuno had, you gained a heightened sense of your own back trail.

Something pricked at that sense now—had been pricking at it all morning, in fact. Cuno had ridden back to take a look but hadn't seen anything.

Still, he couldn't relax.

"You two go on ahead," he told Sandy and Marlene, reining his horse off the trail. "I'm gonna hold back for a while." He tossed Marlene the Arabian's ribbons.

Catching them, she reined up and turned to Cuno, her hat pulled over her forehead, gloved hands holding her reins taut. "What's the matter?"

"Probably nothin', but I'm gonna hang back just to make sure."

"What if we get lost?" she said, her slanted eyes crinkling at the corners. "I've never been through this country before."

"Just keep following this game trail to that pass yonder," Cuno told her, sliding his gaze beyond her to indicate the cleft between two rocky ridges, due north. "According to my map, on the other side there's a little mining town called Canyon City. If you don't see me in a couple of hours, head there."

Sandy sat hipped around in his saddle, looking worried. He'd had his fill of trouble, especially Indian trouble. "What do you think's back there, Cuno?"

"Probably nothin'," he lied, "but out here, you never know. Skedaddle. I'll catch up to you later."

When Marlene, the boy, and the Mexican's Arabian had disappeared over a low rise, their dust sifting behind them, Cuno looked around. In the east rose a low, rocky ridge, its buff sandstone pitted with shadows. In the west, a tree-carpeted mesa arched against the vast blue bowl of the mid-afternoon sky. A large hawk circled lazily over the mesa's boulder-strewn northern slope, a winged mote from this distance.

At the base of the mesa's fir-covered slope, a shallow stream trickled, its sandy banks strewn with rocks and boulders. Deciding the streambed made for good cover, he followed Sandy's and Marlene's tracks up the trail, then doubled back along the stream, and dismounted. Shucking his Winchester, he tied Renegade on a narrow shelf up the mesa's steep, hidden slope. Walking back down to the stream, he hid in a nest of rocks hugging the water.

He'd crouched amongst the rocks for a half hour and was about to leave when a horse's snort rose back along the mesa's slope. His heart increasing its pace, he wheeled to stare straight down the stream meandering along the base of the mesa.

A rustling sound lifted, like something heavy moving through the forest, snapping branches and crushing needles. Moving figures flashed between the trees, and finally six riders slipped out of the woods at the base of the mesa.

One of the riders, a tall man with hair stretched back and thonged in a ponytail, was bare-chested and holding a feathered war lance. He wore only a breechclout; his muscular, copper thighs were bare. The others were clad in combinations of buckskins and calico; one wore a white man's bowler hat over a red bandanna, a bear-tooth necklace hanging down his tattered white shirt with blue pinstripes.

The six Indians were armed with bows and arrows, tomahawks belted around their waists. Some wielded war lances decorated with eagle and hawk feathers. Their faces were streaked and hashed with war paint.

Cuno's fingers dug into his Winchester's stock. These men were part of the group that had raided the farmstead. They'd probably returned for the braves who'd stayed behind to kill the animals, found the bodies, and picked up the trail of Cuno's party.

The leader spoke in what Cuno assumed was Kiowa, and led the group across the stream and up the opposite slope to the game trail that Cuno, Sandy, and Marlene had been following. They paused there, scouring the trail with their eyes, then started moving northward at a slow, purposeful pace.

Cuno watched the Indians disappear up the slow rise. There was no doubt they were dogging him, and no doubt there was only one way to get them off his trail.

Scrambling through the trees on the mesa's slope, he retrieved his horse, rode back down the hill, and gigged the paint north. He rode slowly, trying to make as little noise as possible. If the horse so much as blew or clipped a rock with a shod hoof, the keen-eared Indians would pick it up.

The six riders appeared before him, spread out along the trail. The leader was looking left, apparently reading the sign Cuno had left when he'd doubled back along the stream.

Anxiety tightened the back of his head, and his hands tingled. He had to take them now, before they turned around and saw him.

Too late. The leader had already turned. Pointing, the tall man yelled. The others jerked their heads sharply back along the trail as Cuno leapt from his saddle, slapping his horse's ass with his rifle butt.

"Hee-ya, Renegade! Move!"

The horse dug its rear hooves into the sod and thundered

down the slope. Meanwhile, Cuno raised the rifle to his shoulder and began firing, aiming hastily, loosing as much lead as he could before the Indians had time to notch their arrows or fling their lances.

Over his smoking barrel, he saw one Indian grab his chest and tumble off his horse. Another man's forehead turned red as he, too, was flung from his blanket saddle.

Meanwhile, the four others leapt from their mounts, twisting and turning, pivoting, hollering, notching arrows in midair. They scrambled to their knees, flicking arrows, the feathered shafts sizzling through the air around Cuno's head, tearing into the turf around his feet. As soon as they fired, their hands whipped over their shoulders, grabbing more arrows from their quivers, and notching them—all in a single blink.

Cuno fired two more shots, missing his jostling targets, and bolted right, making for the rocky spur and cover as more arrows whined like bees around his ears.

These Kiowa were good fighters. His odds against such formidable adversaries were slim.

The thought had barely passed through his mind when, just as he reached the slope, he felt a sudden icy burn in his right calf. He bit down hard on his back teeth, ignoring the pain, knowing that to stop would mean getting drilled by one of the arrows pinging off the rocks on either side of him.

Not looking back, squeezing his rifle tight around the breech, he ran up the slope, slipping on the loose scree. He dropped to a knee. An arrow sizzled over his left ear, nicking his cheek. It was all the encouragement he needed to heave himself back up, bolting forward and around a boulder, sitting down with a curse, and clutching the wounded calf from which the hawk-feathered shaft of an arrow extended.

The steel head protruded from his torn jeans on the other side, dripping blood. He stole a look around the boulder, casting his gaze down slope.

The four Kiowa were spread out, making their way up

the butte, arrows notched and held down at their hips, coal-eyed, roughly chiseled faces canted toward the boulder behind which Cuno crouched.

Grunting with pain, he glanced up the slope behind him. There was a shelf about twenty feet up; then the ridge rose more gradually, pocked with cracks and crevices and littered with jagged rocks and boulders. In some places the orange soil gave way to sheer rock, but Cuno thought he could scramble over it.

He had to. There was nowhere else to go.

Quickly, he heaved himself out from the boulder and, crouching, took aim at the Indian wearing the bowler, and fired. The man had seen him and thrown himself right, and the shot went wild.

Meanwhile, Cuno levered off the rest of the rounds in his magazine, then lowered the rifle to watch the four Kiowa scramble back down the slope, taking cover in the grass below the trail.

The first part of his mission accomplished, Cuno crouched again behind the boulder, set his rifle aside, dropped to his ass, and grabbed both ends of the arrow protruding from his calf. Grinding his teeth together, he snapped the arrow in two, and pulled the feathered end from his leg, grunting and cursing with the pain. Fortunately, it was a clean wound, missing the bone, and he was able to stem the blood flow with his neckerchief, knotted four inches above his ankle.

That done, he reloaded his rifle from his cartridge belt and cast a glance back down the rock-strewn butte. The four Kiowa were vague, coppery blurs in the high weeds on the other side of the trail. One was moving to Cuno's right, apparently swinging wide to approach the butte from a greater angle.

Cuno fired three quick shots to hold the Indians at bay, then pivoted, ran out from behind the boulder, and scrambled up the butte, grabbing at rocks with his hands and feet, wheezing against the throbbing in his calf, heaving himself toward the brow.

Behind him, the Indians gave an eager howl. Cuno heard them scrambling up from the grassy slope and begin running up the butte behind him. He was too busy clawing his way up the slope, grabbing at rocks, quickly but gingerly lifting his wounded leg over boulders, to look behind. But by the sounds of raking breath and scuffed stones, he knew they'd spread out on either side of him, trying to overtake him at various angles.

Several paused to loose arrows, which clattered amongst the rocks below and above him. One ripped through the slack shirt beneath his arm and clattered into a rock beneath him. As he pulled himself up and over the crown of the butte, he brought the arrow with him, embedded in his buckskin shirt.

Cuno's leg cried out with grief as he smacked it against a sharp sandstone scarp as he scrambled for cover along the brow of the butte. He yanked the arrow out of his shirt, propped the Winchester on the scree-covered ridge top, lowered his cheek to the stock, and quickly picked out a coppery figure scrambling up the slope directly below.

The gun jumped. The Indian groaned and fell to a knee, dropping his bow. He grabbed his arm and had begun crawling toward a rock for cover, when Cuno fired again. The Indian's head exploded, blood splashing the boulder behind him.

Cuno ducked as a war lance made a whushing sound as it careened toward him from downslope. It split the air a few inches above his head and clattered down the hill behind him. An arrow fanned his cheek as he rose up again and fired four more rounds at moving, brown targets, hitting nothing but rock and gravel, the spanging reports echoing between the ridges.

He was about to squeeze off another round, but held off. The Kiowas had taken cover behind rocks. They were still moving, he saw, working their way up the butte, no doubt intending to get around him, but doing so as they zigzagged behind boulders, virtually out of sight.

Cuno looked around. There was no covering rock within

twenty feet. If the Indians got around him, they'd have a clear shot at him.

Grimacing, he pushed himself to his feet and, holding the Winchester in one hand, made his way down the opposite side of the butte, where cedars and cracked boulders offered cover: For how long, he didn't know. He was hip-high in deep shit. With his wounded calf, he couldn't run far. He just had to hole up and hope he could pick off the Kiowa as they attacked him one at a time.

He scrambled sideways down the slope, limping on the gimpy calf, holding the Winchester out for balance. When he came to the tree line, he paused, sweeping the uneven slope from left to right. On his right and about fifty feet down the hill, he saw what looked like promising cover, and made for it. It turned out to be a natural, semicircular bunker of sorts, four feet tall, with several stunted trees growing out of the mica-flecked rock.

Not bad.

After first making sure he wouldn't be sharing the space with any wild creatures like cougars or diamondbacks, he scrambled over the rocks and hunkered down in the bunker. It smelled faintly of skunk musk and was littered with black, ropy coyote scat. Setting the rifle down and biting his lip, he tightened the bloody neckerchief around the wounded calf, and peered over the rock wall, sweeping the butte top with his gaze.

A brown blur flashed on his right, disappearing behind a nest of cedars. Another man appeared on his far left, the Indian crouching there, his arrow notched, his lime-green bandanna whipping in the breeze.

Cuno ducked down, hoping he hadn't been seen, and grabbed the Winchester. As he quietly levered a shell in the breech and glanced at the line of empty leather shell loops on his cartridge belt, a sickening thought occurred to him.

He was almost out of ammo.

12

CUNO LOADED HIS last six shells into the Winchester. His .45 Colt was already loaded. That gave him twelve shots altogether, more than enough for three white men, but he was dealing with Kiowa who could duck and dodge like phantoms.

He'd have to shoot sparingly.

Scooting out from the rock wall, he expended another glance toward the brow of the butte. The Indian was still crouched beside the rock, notched arrow held at his shoulder, raking his gaze along the slope.

As the man's head turned toward him, Cuno darted back against the wall, grimacing anxiously, hoping he hadn't been seen. Pressing his back against the rocks, squeezing the Winchester in both hands, he ticked off the seconds. When a minute had passed, he dared another look up the butte.

The Indian was no longer at the crest. Spying movement out of the corner of his left eye, Cuno ducked. An arrow whistled through the air two inches above his head, thumping off a rock and clattering around his feet.

Whipping the rifle up, he saw the Kiowa rise off his knees and scramble back behind a boulder, Cuno's two

shots kicking up dust and gravel at his heels. A rock rolled
down the slope behind him, and Cuno turned to see another
Indian skipping down behind a dwarf pine.

Cuno fired, snapping off a branch, then ducked down
behind the bunker, cursing.

He couldn't hold them off for long. He didn't have
enough ammo. Pressing his back against the rocks and listening for movement around him, he decided to kill as
many of the surviving three warriors as he could, and save
the last shot for himself.

He didn't want to end up in some Kiowa camp tonight,
slow-roasted over a hot fire.

He cursed again, rolled his eyes from left to right, watching for movement. It came quickly from his left, the Indian
sprinting down the slope at an angle, hurdling a deadfall
tree. Cuno aimed, fired, and cursed, his slug careening over
the jumping Indian's shoulder just before the warrior
ducked behind a low hummock about thirty yards away.

Meanwhile, a shrill, teeth-gnashing cry pierced the air.

Turning quickly, Cuno saw another redskin storm toward the bunker, crouching as he ran, obsidian hair string-
ing out around his shoulders. Ten feet beyond Cuno—close
enough that Cuno could see his pitted face and wide,
liquid-brown eyes flashing fury—the young warrior
stopped and drew the arrow back, making the willow bow
creak like leather.

Cuno fired first, bringing the rifle up quickly. The brave
released the arrow an instant after Cuno's slug took him
high in the chest. The arrow whacked into the rocks near
Cuno's left knee. As the brave pinwheeled, crying, Cuno
felt something plunge into his right thigh.

Instantly, his whole leg numbed. He twisted, stumbling
and dropping the rifle.

The Indian who'd fired the arrow gave a victorious
whoop and stepped out from his cover, nocking another arrow. Cuno grabbed his Colt and loosed three, careless
shots—shooting out of fury, sheer spite, his adrenaline
spurting through every limb, his leg crying out in pain. The

Indian turned, stumbling, and dove behind a low mound of mangled juniper shrubs, not even grazed.

Cursing himself as well as his predicament, Cuno threw himself back against the rocks, shifting the Colt to his left hand and clutching his right thigh. Around the arrow, blood soaked his jeans, thick and sticky and building in volume.

He groaned with the pain, squeezing the wound closed around the arrow. His face was sweat-basted, and so was his shirt—broad wet swaths down his chest and under his arms. Somewhere he'd lost his hat, and his blond hair was pasted against his scalp.

He was done for. The two remaining Indians had him trapped.

Looking around, he saw that he'd dropped his rifle over the bunker wall. He had only his pistol now, with three shells left in the cylinder.

Two for the Indians. And if that didn't work, one for himself.

He sat there, breathing hard, clutching his wounded thigh with one hand, his pistol in the other, waiting. Time passed, the sun arcing westward, birds and chipmunks chattering in the ravine at the base of the slope. Cuno listened for the Indians but heard nothing.

Apparently, they were waiting him out. He doubted they wanted him to bleed to death. Being Indians, especially Kiowa, they'd want to finish him personally. They were just letting time pass, hoping to catch him off guard.

Above and beyond the pain in his throbbing right leg, Cuno felt grave disappointment that his run had come to an end before he could settle his score with the rancher, Evans, in Julesburg. He'd really hoped he could do that one last thing for July.

He cocked his head and squinted one eye at the sky. The sun was quartering toward the western ridges. It would be dark soon. Maybe that's what the Indians were waiting for, to get the sun behind them. Then they'd rush toward the bunker with arrows nocked.

Cuno would get one. Damn if he wouldn't get at least one.

The thought had barely passed before he saw something move on his left side, about thirty feet away. Knowing one could be trying to distract him while the other charged, Cuno looked to his right in time to see a brown blur as the Indian on that side ran behind a rock.

Cuno jerked another look left, and the Indian there lifted his head above a pine stump, stretched his lips back from his teeth, and gave a whoop not unlike a rebel yell. Laughing, he ducked back behind the stump.

Cuno smiled to himself. The man had been trying to attract his fire, wanting him to waste more ammo, but Cuno had resisted.

"Forget it, you damn savage!" Cuno yelled. "I'm gonna wait until I've got a good solid bead on your forehead, and then I'm gonna blow your brains out!"

The words hadn't died on his tongue before the Indian on his right leapt out from cover, running toward him. Cuno leveled the pistol on him and fired. Again, he missed as the Indian hunkered down behind a low scarp covered with leaves and pine needles, only ten feet away.

Quickly turning, Cuno saw the man on his left making a run toward him, as well. Cuno fired his second-to-last shot. The Indian stopped dead in his tracks, straightening, dropping his bow and arrow straight down as he threw his head back, a bloody smear in his forehead, just above the bridge of his nose.

The Indian dropped to his knees as though cut from strings, fell forward in the rocky soil, shook his head once, jerked a moccasin, and lay still.

Cuno turned back the other way in time to see the other warrior coming at him, bolting off his feet in an arching dive, screaming like a banshee, a tomahawk held blade-forward in his right hand.

Watching the tomahawk's blade winking in the orange light, Cuno lifted his gun. In the back of his mind, he knew he wouldn't get the barrel leveled in time, so he lifted his left hand, trying to block the Indian's blow.

At the same time, a shot rang out.

Vaguely, he was aware of the Indian's savage expression suddenly slackening. The Kiowa bowled into him like a sack of corn thrown from a supply wagon, knocking Cuno onto his back. The Indian lay motionless, his deadweight pressing down on Cuno's chest.

Flat on his back, Cuno blinked his eyes as he looked around.

What the hell?

Hearing footsteps, he tipped his head to peer in the direction from which the last Indian had come. A slight figure hop-skipped down the slope, blond hair bouncing down from a man's felt hat, a rifle held across her chest. Behind Marlene came the boy, carrying his big Remington in both hands, descending the slope with more care than the girl.

They approached until Marlene Stratton was staring down at Cuno, still lying beneath the dead Indian. Cuno stared up at her.

Marlene planted one fist on her hip and set her lips with disgust. "If I could have made a shot like that a few nights ago, I'd be five thousand dollars richer by now."

13

"YOU ALL RIGHT?" Sandy Hilman asked as he hunkered down beside Cuno in the bunker, the boy's eyes bright with worry. He ran his gaze over the wounds and made a face. "That looks bad!"

"I'll be okay," Cuno said with a grin that didn't quite make it to his eyes.

"Boy, do me a favor and try to run Renegade down? He's on the other side of the butte somewhere. Give two sharp whistles." Cuno grimaced as pain spasmed through his bloody, arrow-pierced thigh. "That should bring him."

The boy hesitated, his sweat-streaked face creased with anxiety. He was breathing heavily from the climb over the butte. "You sure you're gonna be all right?"

"I'm sure," Cuno rasped out. He gave him a gentle shove. "Go now!"

Reluctantly, the boy scrambled over the rock wall and began climbing back up the butte. The girl took his place beside Cuno, switching her rifle to her left hand and raking her eyes over the wounds.

Her previous humor had faded without a trace. "We heard the shooting."

"Help me up," Cuno said, clutching her arm.

"You'll never make it up the butte." She shifted her gaze from his leg to his face. "We best wait here for Sandy and Renegade."

Cuno shook his head and pulled against her, climbing to his feet. "More Injuns could have heard the shots."

"You'll never make it with that arrow in—"

She didn't have to finish the sentence. He'd climbed halfway to his feet, winced as the pain bit him hard, numbing his entire right leg. Cursing, his features bathed in sweat, he sat back down against the rocks. "Christ!"

She knelt beside him, gazing at him darkly. Her voice had lost all trace of its customary irony. "We'll wait for Sandy."

He panted, then rasped out, "Dig a bullet out of one of your cartridges."

She scowled. "What?"

"An old trick I learned from my old man when Arapahos attacked our freight wagons. Dig a bullet out of a shell casing. Hurry."

She ejected a shell from her rifle. Her hands trembling, she accepted his knife and began prying the slug from the casing. She dropped the knife once, cursed, and continued. Finally, the lead ball jerked from the brass and tumbled around Cuno's legs.

"Good girl," he said.

Taking the knife back, working quickly, aware that more Indians could be charging down the butte at any moment, he cut off the pointed end of the arrow and split it lengthwise with his knife. His hands trembled from the pain that shot up from his throbbing thigh, making his stomach roll so that he felt like throwing up.

He poured the gunpowder from the casing into the crack, making a good four-inch line.

"What the hell are you doing?" Marlene asked, watching.

"Got a match?"

Her eyes met his, fear mixing with scorn.

He thrust his open palm at her. "Give me a match!"

Exhaling an exasperated breath, she fished a matchbox from her shirt pocket and slapped it into his palm. He fished out a match, scraped it on his cartridge belt. It flared.

He glanced at the flame, steeling himself, swallowed hard. He touched the flame to the furrow he'd plowed in the arrow.

The powder flashed, black smoke puffing, filling the air with its acrid smell. At the same time, cursing loudly, Cuno gave the feathered shaft a fierce yank, forcing himself to keep pulling despite the white-hot pain as the blazing shaft slipped back through the torn muscle and flesh.

The pain was almost unendurable. Still, he didn't stop pulling until the shaft was out. An eye blink after he'd dropped the bloody shaft, his eyes glazed and rolled back in his head.

He slumped back against the rock wall, out like a blown candle.

When he woke, Marlene was tying a strip of cloth the same color as her shirt around his thigh. What was left of her shirt lay beside her on the rocks. She was clad in only her loose undershirt, under which her small, pointed breasts swayed.

Glancing at his face, she saw that his eyes were open. "The bleeding's stopped," she said, tightening the knot over the wound.

"Cauterized all the way through," Cuno grunted, pushing himself onto his elbows to inspect the wound. "We got to get over the mountain . . . meet Sandy on the other side . . ."

"No."

"Yes," he grunted again, grabbing the rocks and heaving himself to his feet.

"You're gonna open those wounds again, and—"

"If we don't get out of here, there's gonna be plenty more savages where those came from." Brusquely, he draped an arm around her shoulder and hobbled over the bunker's low wall.

"If there were more Indians around, they'd be here," she protested, grunting under his weight.

"We wait a few minutes, they will be."

"What?"

He sighed painfully as he stooped to retrieve his rifle, then straightened and pointed a finger to the northeast, beyond the furry, rocky humps of hills and buttes, where a string of riders cantered through a ravine. They were mere horse-and-rider-shaped specks from this distance, but specks with long hair and feathered lances.

"Why do you always have to be right!" she exclaimed, throwing an arm around his waist and guiding him up the butte.

He nearly passed out several times on his journey up the mountain, once after he'd kicked a rock with his bad leg. The pain shot up and down the leg and into his belly, like razor-edged javelins, the world darkening before his eyes.

They were halfway down the other side when he saw Sandy sitting his pinto pony on the valley floor. Renegade stood behind him, his reins in Sandy's hands. Marlene's dappled mustang and the Arabian were tethered to a shrub. The four horses and the boy were watching Marlene and Cuno clamber down the slope, Cuno kicking his bad leg out, using his rifle as a cane.

"How you feelin', Cuno?" the boy asked.

Cuno paused beside Renegade, pressing his face against the fender of his saddle, biting down hard against the unrelenting pain, fighting off the weakness and nausea. "Peachy," he raked out. To Marlene, he said, "Help me up."

Sandy quickly dismounted, and when he and Marlene had Cuno in his saddle, Cuno heeled Renegade into a trot, gritting his teeth as the horse's gait wracked his body. He knew he couldn't take much more jarring before his thigh opened up again, but there was no choice. With the Indians behind them, he either rode or died and got the boy and the girl killed in the process.

He made Sandy and Marlene ride ahead while he rode drag, keeping an eye on their back trail. He was in no condition for another fight, but if the Indians caught up to them, he might hold them off for a few minutes, until Marlene and Sandy made it to Canyon City, which his map had told him lay on the other side of Canyon Pass.

"Go, boy," he urged. Sandy had slowed for him as they descended a long grade between towering, rocky cliffs. The boy had hipped around in his saddle, regarding Cuno with wide-eyed concern. "Keep going! I'm coming!"

They rode another four hard miles. Cuno paused on a rise and regarded their back trail, his hand squeezing the pounding thigh wound closed. He thought they'd outdistanced the Kiowa by a couple miles.

Relief washed through him when they finally brought their horses to a stop on a hill overlooking a deep canyon. At the bottom of the canyon nestled the town—a boomtown not unlike the others he'd seen. A couple of main drags sitting perpendicular to each other sported tall, false-fronted buildings of new yellow lumber. Beyond lay the log shacks and tents, filthy canvas snapping in the breeze.

Reinforced mountain wagons on high, iron wheels milled about the deep-rutted streets, while bearded men clad in baggy duck trousers and thick, flat-soled boots tramped about the boardwalks. Signs for drinks, women, billiards, and mining equipment stood or hung virtually everywhere.

Exhausted, he lifted his gaze to the scree-covered, pine-dotted slopes around him. Cuno saw the broad swaths of broken rock tailing out from wood-framed burrows. Inside such caves, men picked and prodded the mountain for golden fortunes.

Rumbling lifted behind him, and he swung his head around. A stout platform dray, its bed loaded with raw ore, thundered through the pines along the slope, turning onto the main trail without slowing. The four mules in the traces galloped with their ears back, the burly miner in the driver's seat whipping a blacksnake over their backs.

Renegade gave a start, catching Cuno off guard. Unable to grip the saddle with his right thigh, Cuno tumbled out of the saddle, sprawling onto the trail. Marlene and Sandy dismounted in a hurry, and half-dragged, half-carried Cuno to the narrow gully along the trail seconds before the ore wagon broiled past, whipping the air and making the ground quake.

"Get the hell outta the road, pilgrim!" the burly driver roared as he cracked the whip. "It's damn near happy hour at the Canyon Gal!"

The man guffawed as the wagon thundered down the rocky slope, whipped around a bend, and vanished over the slope's brow toward the town. For several seconds, the air and the ground shuddered in its wake.

Crouched beside Cuno in the gully, Marlene yelled an unladylike epithet toward the vanished wagon—one which only Cuno and Sandy could hear. Cuno lay on his side, gripping his thundering thigh in both fists, muttering curses of his own.

"You're bleeding again!" Marlene admonished.

"Help me up."

"You need a doctor."

He shook his head. "No doctor. Just rest." He clutched at the thigh while inspecting it, back teeth grinding together. The wounds had opened, adding fresh blood to the jelly on his jeans. It hurt even worse than before, making trees, rocks, and the trail swirl before his eyes.

"If you don't see a doctor, you'll bleed dry," Marlene exclaimed as she and Sandy helped him to his feet. Sandy held Renegade's reins.

"All right," Cuno said, flailing for his saddle horn. "But let's try to stay out of sight as much as we can." In any mining town, they'd find men who thought themselves equal to the task of landing a five-thousand-dollar bounty. The wanted circulars bearing his description and rough sketch had been well circulated.

He followed Sandy and Marlene down the trail and into the outskirts of the town, making an effort to keep his head up and not draw attention to himself. It was a difficult proposition. The tipping, lunging world kept turning gray before his eyes, and several times he nearly passed out. He was glad the sun had set behind the towering ridges, from which issued the occasional reports of dynamite blasts. The purple shadows concealed his face and bloody pants leg.

They reined up near a livery corral where the muddy mountain trail emerged from the log shacks and tents and entered the town.

"Marlene," Cuno said. "Sandy and I'll wait here while you look for a doctor's office."

The girl nodded and gigged her horse down the street, swinging her head from left to right, looking for the shingle of a sawbones. Men gawked at her from wagons and board-walks; it was no doubt unusual to see a girl dressed in men's rough trail garb in these parts. The only other women were scantily clad in pink or rose satin and black lace, touting their fleshy wares from balconies or boardwalks fronting saloons.

Marlene returned a few minutes later, waking Cuno from a teeth-gnashing doze, head tipped over Renegade's neck. "Found a place," she said, slipping the reins from Cuno's loose grip and starting around the livery barn's rear paddock filled with mules. "We can get to it from the alley."

Cuno gripped the saddle horn as Renegade trotted after the girl's mustang. Seeing two men standing in the pad-dock, brushing the mules and regarding the three newcom-ers curiously, Cuno lowered his head, gave his hat brim a cursory pinch, and turned away.

With five thousand dollars on your head—a veritable El Dorado to most fortune hunters—the last place you wanted to find yourself was in a goddamn mining town.

14

THEY RODE THROUGH the trash-littered alley, the backs of wood buildings on their left, a line of brush sheathing a riverbed on their right. A piano clattered in one of the taverns. They startled a man and a pleasure girl behind a woodpile, the woman giving a half grunt, half scream of surprise.

As the plump redhead rearranged her skirts, the man buttoned his pants, flushing and snarling, and headed for a tavern's back door flanked with empty whiskey barrels. Frowning at the intruders who'd cost her the going rate for a quick poke in a mining camp, she straightened the tattered pink feathers in her hair and slouched toward the saloon.

When Cuno felt Renegade stop—his eyes were closed— he heard Marlene order Sandy to stay with the horses. With Marlene's help, Cuno slipped clumsily out of the leather and climbed a staircase running along the outside of a two-story building, the steps squawking and creaking under his boots. The wood smelled of fresh pine. The thickening wood smoke wafting from the chimneys was thick with the tang of pine resin, as well.

Marlene knocked on the door at the top of the stairs. When there was no reply, she knocked again, holding Cuno up with one arm. He'd propped a hand on the rail to his right and was fighting his eyes open. Surveying the alley beside the stairs, he was grateful to see no one, hearing only the muffled din from the saloons running up and down the main drag.

Marlene knocked again, breathing hard with the effort of holding Cuno. She felt relief when she heard footsteps growing in volume, saw the windowed door open. A short, stocky man with mussed gray hair and a bushy gray mustache stood framed in the doorway, frowning. His brown eyes were rheumy.

He wore a silk shirt and a wool vest under a bib stained with wine. His breath was stained with the alcohol, as well. Bread crumbs adhered to his lips and mustache, and he held part of a roast beef sandwich, a bite of which he was still chewing, in his right hand.

"You the doc?" Marlene asked.

The man nodded, swallowing and taking Cuno's measure, deep lines etched around his glinting fish eyes. "I'm Doc Romer," the man said in a thick, gravelly voice. "What you got here?"

"He has two arrow wounds in his right leg," Marlene gasped. She wrestled Cuno through the door as the doctor shuffled back, nearly tripping over his own feet.

"Looks like he's lost a lotta blood," Romer said darkly, again eyeing Cuno's denims. He shut the door and turned into a small room with a battered rolltop desk, a small coal burner, a couple of Windsor chairs, and a file cabinet. "This way."

He set his bib and sandwich on the desk and, dusting his hands on his baggy trousers, walked into an even smaller room rife with the smell of carbolic acid and alcohol. Marlene followed him, guiding Cuno with both arms around his waist, tripping over his feet.

"Get him on the table there," the doctor ordered with an

air of grim imposition, as though he'd been called away from something far more important than doctoring some pilgrim.

Cuno was already sagging against the examining table, eyes fluttering, feet shuffling like a drunk's, his pale, sweat-soaked features etched with pain. Marlene gentled him onto the table, then lifted his feet until he was stretched out on his back, groaning, sweat runneling his pain-curled cheeks.

The doctor produced a curved scissors from a preparation table, knocking a jar of other sharp instruments over in the process. Muttering a curse, he ambled over to the examination table, and leaned close to inspect the wounds, squinting and wrinkling his nose. Muttering another curse, he began slicing through the neckerchief tied around the wound in Cuno's calf.

His halting movements and unsteady hands did nothing to build Marlene's confidence, but she doubted she'd find another sawbones in the mining camp. Most camps were lucky if they had one, let alone a sober one.

"Is this Arapaho handiwork?" Romer asked.

"Kiowa," Marlene said.

The doctor clucked his tongue. He'd removed the bandage over Cuno's thigh and was cutting away the trousers, the scissors faltering on the tough, blood-soaked denim.

"He doesn't look like a miner," Romer said, prodding.

"He's not." Marlene knew her cryptic reply wouldn't satisfy the curious doctor. She sagged back against the wall, as exhausted as she'd ever been, and tried to dream up a background for her and Cuno, but, too weary to think of anything, she let it go.

The old sawbones gave her a curious, sidelong glance, then went back to cutting.

Cuno was out, eyelids fluttering, head shaking slowly from side to side.

"What're your names?" the doctor pressed after a minute, his offhand tone belying his suspicious curiosity.

"No offense, Doc," Marlene said with an impatient sigh,

"but that's none of your business. Just fix my friend up, and we'll be on our way."

The doctor glanced up at her, his red nose turning redder. "No reason to get your underpants in a twist, young lady," Romer said. "I was just tryin' to make conversation."

"I'm too tired for conversation."

"Are you too tired to give me a hand?"

She stared at him.

"See that whiskey bottle over there? Pop the cork and force as much down your friend's throat as you can get. I'm gonna have to clean and stitch these wounds, and he'll need to be out."

"Whiskey, huh?" Marlene said with a caustic snort, reaching for the bottle. "I thought medics used laudanum or chloroform these days."

"Or cocaine," the doctor said. "You know how much that fancy stuff costs and how much miners are willin' to pay for medical services?" Romer dropped the scissors on the preparation table with a mirthless chuff, and headed for the door. "Whiskey works just as good."

While Romer pumped water and stoked the coal stove in the other room, Marlene lifted Cuno's head with one arm and hoisted the bottle to his lips with the other. He took several liberal slugs, dribbling only a little down his chin. Marlene gave him a minute. Hearing the water boiling in the other room, she tried to get him to drink more. He gave his head a single, resolute shake and rasped, "No more."

"Our friend good an' soused?" Romer asked, returning with a basin of steaming water and several cloths thrown over his arm. He stumbled and glared down at his feet, muttering curses.

Marlene wanted to say that Cuno was nearly as drunk as his doctor, but decided to hold her tongue. Without the man's help, Cuno would no doubt bleed to death or die of infection.

Marlene grunted in the affirmative.

Romer popped the cork on the whiskey bottle, winked at Marlene, said, "It is only ethical for a doctor to sample his own medicine."

Marlene sneered as he tipped back the whiskey until his Adam's apple had bobbed twice. Then he lowered it with a raspy sigh, corked it, wrung out a rag in the steaming water, and set to work cleaning the wound that had turned Cuno's exposed thigh to a puddle of jellied blood and skin the color of an overripe chokecherry.

"I'm not going to bother suturing the wounds," Romer said when, after a half hour had passed, he'd finished the cleaning.

"What do you mean you're not going to suture them?" Marlene asked, frowning hard.

"Both wounds are relatively clean. I'll put some salve on them and wrap them. That should do."

"They won't break open?"

"If I thought they'd break open, I'd suture them, wouldn't I?" Romer snapped defensively, avoiding her gaze.

Marlene studied him, angry and perplexed. Drunk as he was, she had to admit he looked and sounded like he knew what he was doing. Still, something bothered her about his not suturing the wounds.

"How long until he'll be able to ride?" she asked.

Romer was wrapping clean, white cloth around the calf. His hands were shaking slightly, Marlene noted. The look in his eyes, an enervated perplexity, told her the shakes weren't due to the alcohol alone. He seemed nervous, rushed, in spite of the fact he'd been here alone when she'd rapped on the door. No other patients awaited his services.

"Oh, I'd say a couple weeks."

"That's too long," Marlene said.

"Young lady," Romer said patronizingly, "your friend's leg has been by pierced by Kiowa arrows. If they'd struck the bone, he'd probably lose the leg. Why don't you run along?"

"What?"

"He'll spend the night here."

Marlene wasn't sure why she didn't like the idea. "Why?"

"So I can keep an eye on him," the doctor said, voice pinched with impatience. "That sweat isn't from exhaustion alone—it's fever. Mrs. Evinrude's boardinghouse is just over the hill on the south side of town. She's cheap, and if you don't have money, she'll let you do her dishes or empty her slop pails."

Marlene stood regarding the tipsy sawbones skeptically.

Romer looked at Marlene with anxious, impatient eyes, his face flushed. "Out!"

Marlene regarded Cuno, uncertain, befuddled, anxious. Looking at the doctor again, she saw a definite subversive cast to his gaze.

Finally, she said, "All right. I'll be back in the morning."

Then she wheeled, started out the door, turned back to glance again at Cuno, then let herself out the door over the stairs.

She paused on the landing, looked around. The sun had fallen, cloaking Canyon City in near darkness. Haltingly, she started down the stairs. Something didn't feel right, but she wasn't sure what it was.

"How is he?" It was Sandy. He'd moved out of the brush on the other side of the alley and stood gazing at Marlene with concern.

"I think he'll be all right," she mumbled, brows still furled.

"He stayin' at the doc's tonight?"

"I reckon." Marlene walked into the shadows across the alley as though in a dream, her head down. Absently, she kicked a tin can.

"What's wrong?" Sandy said, coming up behind her.

"I don't know." She turned to him, an idea forming itself. "Where're the horses?"

Sandy's face showed confusion and alarm. He jerked his head at the brush lining the alley. "Yonder in the wash."

"Good." Marlene grabbed his arm, jerked him down the alley, led him behind a woodshed.

"What are we doin'?" Sandy demanded.

"Waitin' right here."

"For what?"

"Shhh."

Marlene waited, her back to the shed, glancing around the corner. Sandy stood beside her, and she hushed his occasional queries and complaints with a brusque hand on his arm or an elbow in the ribs.

The din from the saloons was growing, voices mixing with the pianos. Farther up the alley, a woman sang with a piano and a fiddle—a somber, off-key voice straining to be more than it was. Marlene knew that when enough whiskey had been consumed, the voice would be drowned by heckles and catcalls, and she allowed herself a wry smile.

A quarter hour had passed when a door clicked shut in the direction of the doctor's office. Shoes clattered on the squeaky stairs, and the doctor's short silhouette appeared, wearing a jacket and a bowler, a glowing cigar protruding from his lips.

At the bottom of the stairs, he turned sharply and headed toward the main drag, walking fast.

Marlene squeezed Sandy's elbow. "Wait here."

Before he could protest, Marlene ran out from behind the shed and paused at the bottom of the steps, peering toward the main street. The doctor's squat silhouette disappeared around a store corner.

Marlene ran to the corner of the Drug Emporium, stopped, and edged her gaze up the street.

The doctor waited for a grocery wagon to pass, then stepped off the boardwalk. He crossed the street and walked along the north-facing buildings, weaving through the men drinking outside the saloons, several gaudily dressed women clinging to their elbows.

Marlene waited, staying out of sight. The doctor walked quickly, pumping his short legs, not pausing to tip his hat to the ladies. Finally, he strode past a saddle shop, then turned into a saloon, gaslit batwings swinging behind him.

Marlene's heart quickened. Turning, she ran back to the alley and called for Sandy, who came running.

"Come on, shavetail," she said as she mounted the stairs to the doctor's office, moving fast.

"What's going on?" Sandy asked as he marched up the steps behind her.

"We have to get Cuno outta town."

"Why?"

"I have a funny feelin' about that sawbones."

She stopped at the top of the stairs and tried the knob. The fact that it wasn't locked gave her relief, but it also told her that the doctor intended to return quickly. That, in turn, told her that her suspicions were correct. The doctor had recognized Cuno and had gone off to find someone willing and able to share in the bounty.

That was probably another reason why Romer hadn't troubled himself with suturing Cuno's wounds. Why waste time on a dead man?

Romer had left a lamp burning on the battered rolltop. Marlene paused, giving a start as she saw a man's silhouette standing before the table in the examining room, stooped over, clutching the table as though to a life raft.

"Cuno?"

"Hunh?" he said thickly. Startled, he turned and stumbled, nearly fell.

"We have to light a shuck," Marlene said, hurrying to him but keeping her voice low.

"I know." Cuno grabbed her arm for balance. "I saw the way he ... stummied ... studied me," he stuttered. "He's seen a flier, all right." He shook his head. "Damn, I'm tip-tipsy."

Marlene leaned into him, taking his weight.

She turned to Sandy. "Bring the horses. I'll help him down the stairs."

"You get the horses," Sandy retorted. "I'm stronger— I'll help him down the stairs."

"Go! Move!"

Sandy chuffed angrily, turned, bolted out the front door,

and clattered down the steps. Marlene draped Cuno's left arm around her shoulders and guided him onto the landing.

"Easy," she said, guiding him down the steps, breathing heavily against his weight. "Don't want those wounds to start bleeding."

Cuno didn't use the right leg at all. He hopped down each step, one step at a time, panting and groaning as the javelins again shot up his leg and into his gut.

When they made the alley, Sandy was standing there with all four sets of reins in his hands.

Marlene was guiding Cuno to Renegade when a man's voice stopped her cold. She jerked her head toward the main street.

"Where you going?" It was Romer.

The doctor and four other men—tall, broad-chested miners—were heading toward them, walking fast.

15

AWKWARDLY, CUNO RIPPED his Colt from his holster and squeezed off three erratic shots, then watched as the five silhouettes scattered and dove for cover, yelling.

"Mount up and ride!" Cuno shouted, grabbing at his saddle horn. Drunk and seeing two of everything, he missed the horn and plunged against the horse, which whinnied and sidestepped, pitching at the sudden shots. Somehow, Cuno got his left boot in a stirrup and, with Marlene pushing from behind, pulled himself into the saddle.

"Marlene, fork leather!" Cuno shouted, triggering two more rounds to hold the doctor and his cohorts at bay, hitting little but air.

Renegade skitter-hopped in a rough circle. Whipping his head around, Cuno saw that Marlene and Sandy were mounted.

A second later, they both gigged their horses into fast gallops down the alley, leaning low over their saddle horns. Cuno triggered another shot toward the doctor and his men, then spurred Renegade after Marlene and Sandy, wincing as his right leg slapped the horse's side with every lunge.

Shoving the pain from his mind, Cuno urged Renegade ahead while watching the horseback figures of Marlene and Sandy dancing ahead of him, weaving around privies and stacked cordwood.

Guns clapped behind him. A bullet sizzled over his back, and Renegade's muscles contracted as the slug whined past his head. Close on the heels of the first bullet, another tore over Cuno and thumped into a chicken coop to his left, evoking several indignant squawks from inside.

"Get that son of a bitch!" Dr. Romer yelled behind him.

The doctor yelled something else, the words sharp with anger but swallowed by distance and drowned by Renegade's pounding hooves.

"Son of a bitch!" Cuno griped. What was the world coming to when even doctors were out for your hide?

As he swung Renegade right, tracing an arc around the livery paddock, he saw Sandy halt his pinto and look back.

"Don't stop! Keep riding! Follow Marlene!"

The boy jerked back around, elbows winging up from his sides as he slapped the reins and dug his heels into his horse's flanks. He galloped after Marlene, who had turned right on the main street, heading back the way they'd come.

It was the only route from town they were familiar with.

As they galloped, Cuno gritted his teeth, hoping against hope that his wounds didn't start bleeding again. It was entirely possible, for the doctor had done a rush job, seeing no reason to waste time and energy on a man he was going to soon kill.

Cuno was aware of figures pausing along both sides of the street to observe the three racing riders. As he left the business district and approached the outlying cabins and tents set willy-nilly about the rabbit brush and wild mahogany, he saw a huge man—a literal giant—on a behemoth buckskin horse, raising the sledge of his right fist. At first, Cuno thought he was hallucinating, but a second look validated the man's presence.

"Goddamn ye to hell!" the giant's voice boomed like freight cars coupling. "Ye damn near run me over!"

He was yelling at Marlene and Sandy. Hearing Cuno's thundering hooves, he turned sharply. Cuno couldn't see his face, only the immense silhouette in the bear-hide tunic, but there was no mistaking the voice even through the thumps and clumps of Renegade's feet.

"Slow your asses down, ye fuckin' sons o' bitches!"

It was Ruben Pacheca. It had to be. Cuno had never met the man, but he'd heard of him. He hoped Pacheca's presence in Canyon City was a coincidence; all he needed was one of the most formidable bounty hunters on the frontier on his ass, in addition to everyone else.

Cuno galloped on past the lantern-lit whiskey tents and hog pens where pleasure girls entertained the rock farmers who'd strolled down from the upper slopes. At the frayed edge of the settlement, where the trail rose into the mountains, Marlene had halted her horse. Sandy halted his pinto now, too, and turned to watch Cuno approach, slumped in his saddle.

"Where we going? What are we doing?" Marlene asked, breathless, as Cuno checked Renegade down to a walk.

Cuno spit copper-tasting phlegm, clutching the bandage around his throbbing thigh. The alcohol had dulled the pain, but not completely. It also made his thoughts heavy and muddy. He shook his head.

"I don't know. Just ride. Lead the way till we find a place to light. I figure we have a few minutes on them. If they come for us, they'll probably need to saddle horses."

Marlene nodded, then wheeled her horse around, urging it up the slope through pines and aspens. Sandy followed, and Cuno brought up the rear. As he rode, his head hung to his chest. He was only vaguely aware of their serpentine course. He didn't know where they were going, doubted Marlene did, but he didn't care.

He wanted only to get somewhere safe and to sleep.

A gun cracked behind him. The bullet whistled over his head, and Renegade jerked, lunging sideways with alarm.

"Keep going," he yelled to Sandy and Marlene—vague, shifting shapes ahead of him.

He turned Renegade off the trail and reined in behind a towering pine. Turning down the trail, he heard hoofbeats of three, maybe four riders. A moment later, he saw the first rider approaching at a lunging gallop, elbows raised high. The gun in his right hand flashed and barked once more.

Trying to swim up from his alcohol fog, Cuno raised his revolver and stared down the barrel. Slowly, the two im-ages of the single rider closed together, and Cuno fired.

The man gave a grunt and tumbled down the opposite side of his horse. The horse stopped, pitched with a whinny, swung around, and headed back the way it had come, nearly colliding with the rider storming up from behind.

Cuno picked the rider's shadow from the enclosing darkness, and fired. The man cursed and returned fire, his pistol geysering flames. The slung whanged into the pine before Cuno. Cuno fired again, but the man had already swung around and was riding back the way he'd come.

Hoofs thumped to Cuno's left. Turning that way, he saw Marlene riding up, Spencer in hand.

"Think I discouraged 'em," Cuno said, "for now."

He gigged Renegade out of the trees. Marlene turned her own horse around and she and Cuno rode up to where Sandy was waiting by a large boulder on the right side of the trail.

"Let's keep moving," Cuno ordered. "As much room as we can put between us and Canyon City, the better."

Marlene took the lead again, and Cuno drooped in his saddle, following, catching occasional glimpses of Sandy riding ahead. Occasionally, when he lifted his head to look around, a narrow path appeared beneath him, winding through deep forest, milky moonlight filtering through the leafy canopy.

At one point, he turned sharply left, climbed a steep grade on a narrow game trail. He threaded an escarpment of strewn granite boulders, climbed still higher, and en-tered a clearing bathed in moonlight and walled with black forest against a violet sky brushed with cream.

An owl dipped low, making Renegade start; then the

horse continued following Sandy, only a half-dozen feet off the pinto's tail. The horses wheezed from the thin-air climb, their hooves thudding heavily in the springy, dew-dappled grass.

Cuno's eyes drooped closed. He felt the saddle horn lightly punch his chest. He didn't know how much time had passed before he heard Marlene's voice, as if from far away.

"Let's get him inside."

"What is this?" Sandy asked.

"A cabin. What's it look like?"

"Whose?"

"How the hell should I know? Looks abandoned, though."

A hand grasped Cuno's arm. He opened his eyes, jerking his head up. Only then did he realize his horse had stopped. Blinking, he looked around, saw a low-slung cabin nestled against the woods, the moonlight limning the weeds on its sod roof.

He felt as though a light were being slowly turned down in his head as he slid from the saddle, gentle hands easing him to the ground. Then he stumbled, with Marlene and Sandy's help, through the grass, up and over a step, and into a dark, enclosed space smelling of skunk and must and old hides.

He was eased onto a creaking cot or a bunk. Someone jerked one boot off, then another, and then a blanket was thrown over him, eased up to his chin. The lamp in his head guttered out, but flickered back to life as someone gently lifted his head, then released it onto something soft.

The lamp went out. He spun downward into a hot soup of half-formed images. July was there, beckoning to him across a broad lake cloaked in morning mist. His father drove a freight wagon through a storm of Indian arrows. His mother stood in a barren room, hands clasped before her, a sad expression pulling her lips down as she told Cuno how sorry she was for dying on him.

And then there was Corsica Landreau, his father's second wife, lying as Cuno had seen her last—dead in a pool of fresh blood, raped and murdered by the hide hunter, Rolf Anderson. Dead as she was, she quirked an odd smile, asking him to add another log to the kitchen stove, for she felt a tremendous chill of a sudden.

Amidst all the images, there was the lingering sensation of bathing in burning steam. The moist heat was in-escapable, no matter how hard he tried to swim or thrash out of it.

Finally, the heat abated. He opened his eyes.

He was on a cot in a small, low-roofed cabin. Midday light angled through two sashed windows, revealing the crevices and the stones embedded in the hard-packed earthen floor. A peeled-log center post stood a few feet away, hung with traps and chains and braided leather straps. There was a small table and one other cot covered with a rumpled Army blanket. Several blankets and a familiar sad-dle lay on the floor against the wall opposite the door.

Lines burrowed into his forehead as he tried to remem-ber where he was and how he'd gotten here.

Footsteps sounded outside. Instinctively, Cuno looked around for his Colt, saw the holster and cartridge belt hanging from a rough-hewn chair on the other side of the table, a good seven feet away.

With a grunt, he shoved up on an elbow. As he slid his left leg off the cot, the cabin door opened. A girl appeared in a green plaid shirt, blue jeans, and a wide, brown belt. The jeans clung to her long legs—slender but with wom-anly curves. The toes of the boots curled back upon them-selves. The sleeves of the shirt were rolled to her elbows, revealing the sleeves of a shabby, gray undershirt. Her dusty blond hair was pulled back in a ponytail. Her bright blue eyes slanted with feline cunning.

Marlene.

The name slipped home like a steel tongue in an old belt hole.

"'Bout time you're coming around. The shavetail and me were going to give you one more day, then leave you to the mercy of the griz that's been prowling around."

Cuno cleared his throat. "How long I been out?"

"Three nights. This is the fourth day."

She strode across the room, sat beside him on the narrow, webbed-hide cot, and placed a hand on his forehead. "The fever broke last night."

Cuno squirmed. "I gotta piss like a Tennessee plow pony."

Marlene stood. "Come on, then," she said. "The maid's fresh out of chamber pots."

He flexed his arms, pressed his hands against the cot. "Don't know if I can get up."

"Sure, you can. You need exercise before you turn to stone." Marlene tossed the two blankets off him, revealing his naked legs, the right one boasting a fresh, clean bandage over the calf, another over the thigh.

He made a face as he rose on his elbows. "What's that smell?"

"The best healing salve you'll find—yarrow root, pine sap, comfrey, pennyroyal, and star moss. I found it out in the woods, and boiled it up outside."

"Stinks like hell!"

"My granny used it on all of us kids' cuts and bruises, and she never lost one—from infection, anyway." Marlene extended her hand to him. "You getting up or you gonna pee in bed?"

With her help, he climbed to his feet, his bones cracking, his muscles straining like those of an old man's, but he was happy to note more stiffness than pain.

He paused on the other side of the threshold, blinking against the clean mountain light. He enjoyed the cool, dry, pine-scented air caressing his face. A squirrel scolded a camp-robber jay in a big pine to his left.

It felt damn good to be alive.

Looking around, he saw all the horses but Sandy's tied to a picket line in lush grass at the edge of the clearing.

"Where in the hell are we, anyway?" he asked Marlene.

"Somewhere northeast of Canyon City," Marlene said, standing beside him in the crisp sunlight. "There's a lake to the east, an old mine to the west, and behind us a rocky cliff. The cabin must've belonged to a trapper not too long ago. Probably driven out by miners."

Cuno's swollen bladder pushed him out away from the cabin, one arm draped over Marlene's shoulders, the other yanking down the waist band of his underpants. He paused by a small piñon and let go with a relieved sigh.

"Ahhh, that feels good."

He glanced at her. She was staring down at him with a funny little smile on her lips.

"Hey, you're gonna stop the flow."

"Can I hold it?"

"What? No. Turn away."

"Oh, come on." She gazed down at his member with a delighted smile, color rising in her fair, smooth, lightly freckled cheeks. She reached out to grab it. He slapped her hand.

"Hey, stop that."

"Oh, please?" she beseeched. "I've always wanted to aim one."

"Get away."

She reached down and grabbed him gently. He didn't have much choice but to let her. Trying to pull away would only send him groundward on his bad leg.

It seemed to take him forever to purge his bladder and, in spite of his self-consciousness at having a woman share in so private a matter, he inwardly admitted to a strangely sensual pleasure. Her hand was gentle and warm. When he was down to dribbles, she shook it for him, giggling like a girl with her first doll.

"Oh, my," she said with ironic surprise, aiming him around with her fingers, "you must've had as much fun as I did."

It had been fun, but his leg was starting to grieve him, and he was tiring fast.

"Cut it out," he said, slapping her hand away and buttoning his pants. "Help me back inside."

"Tired?"

"A little. I'll sleep the rest of the today and tonight, and we'll head out tomorrow."

She guided him back to the cabin. "You're gonna need another three, four days before you're ready to ride."

"Not a chance. I have to get to Julesburg. Where's Sandy?"

"Checking our traplines."

He shuttled her a puzzled look.

"I found several traps layin' around. We're gonna need trail supplies before we head out again, and I thought I could sell some plews."

He winced as they crossed the threshold and headed for his cot. "Where'd you learn how to trap?"

"My grandpappy was a Rocky Mountain trapper back when beaver pelts were still worth something back East. He taught me how to set traps when I was growin' up, figured we might have to go back to it again someday."

Cuno sat down on the cot with a sigh. As she lifted his legs, he gazed at her admiringly. Pretty but tough, she'd done and seen it all. She reminded him a little of July that way. At once earthy and sexy, singularly sensual, arousing his deepest desires.

"Forget about it," she said, raising her eyes, finding his own eyes on the shirt at which her small, firm breasts pushed, the nipples protruding in a way that tickled his loins. She smiled a smoky, cockeyed smile. "You'll have me again soon"—she leaned down and kissed him sweetly on the lips—"but now you need your rest."

16

IN ROOM TWELVE of the Canyon City Inn, Ruben Pacheca thrashed between the spread legs of a rusty-haired whore named Eve.

The bedposts pounded the floor like train pistons, rattling the windows, while the headboard slammed the wall with thunderous, staccato reports, like homemade firecrackers. A gas lamp tingled musically. The drawers in the room's sole dresser shook.

Eve lay all but buried beneath the naked giant, her protesting screams lost beneath his curses and groans. As she pummeled his back with her heels, scratched his neck and shoulders with her fingernails, her face bunched with misery, Pacheca lifted his chin to the wall. His ugly, bearded face was made uglier by a purple swelling over his left jaw. His red-rimmed eyes were drawn with an insane mix of pain, anger, and frustration.

"Goddamn, woman—*satisfy me!*" he raged.

Stopping suddenly, he rolled onto his right elbow. With his left hand, he grabbed her chin, her face appearing doll-sized in his massive paw. *"Satisfy me!"* he wailed again, shaking her, threatening to squeeze her face to powder.

Chopping his hand, she jerked her head free and cried, *"I-I caaaan't!"*

Pacheca's face turned brick red mottled with violet as he ground his jaws together until his teeth cracked audibly. He swept his left hand behind his right shoulder and brought it forward in a vicious arc, the knuckles connecting soundly with the girl's face.

Eve groaned as she flew from the bed, arms and legs akimbo, and hit the floor with a slap and a thump. Pacheca moved to the edge of the bed, preparing to stand. He froze when the door swung open to reveal a short, broad-shouldered man with a scraggly beard and a bartender's apron. His Mexican features were pinched with anger as he shuttled his gaze from Eve, sobbing on the floor, to Pacheca.

"What you do to my whore, big man?" he scolded.

"She's worthless!" Pacheca boomed, not bothering to cover himself. "Like fuckin' a cold blanket!"

The giant winced and slapped a hand to his swollen cheek. He felt like he was sucking a billiard ball.

Ignoring Eve, who was slumped over on her knees, her cheek pressed to the floor, sobbing, the Mexican bartender stepped toward Pacheca, slitting his eyes and shaking his head.

"It ain't no whore you need, big man. You need dentist. Ouch!" He gave his head another shake at the giant's fiery, lumpy jowl. "That looks bad. It hurts, no?"

"Hurts like hell," Pacheca muttered thickly around the swelling, sitting on the edge of the bed, regarding the crying whore with disdain.

He'd hoped the whore and some whiskey would take his mind off the throbbing tooth, which had begun aching three days ago. At first, the pain was a dull ache, and he'd been able to ignore it. Yesterday, however, it had begun grieving him with a vengeance. The whiskey had worked for a while, and then he'd decided to try a whore.

Sitting in a hotel saloon, he grabbed the first one he saw, threw her over a shoulder, and carried her upstairs.

A dentist hadn't occurred to him. He'd never visited one before. His teeth had never grieved him. It was this damn civilized living that rotted the teeth, the same way it rotted your bones, shriveled your lungs and your heart, diseased your mind.

He should have stayed in the mountains. . . .

"Look what you did to Eve," the bartender/pimp said, extending his arm and open palm at the girl. "She's my best whore. If you put her out of commission, you have to pay."

Ignoring the man, Pacheca reached for his shirt. "Where's the dentist?"

"Ain't no dentist in Canyon City. Have to see Doc Romer. He take care of you, but he's pricey. Twenty-five cents a tooth." The bartender shrugged. "It is a boom-town, no?"

Pacheca tugged his shirt on and reached for his boots.

"Come on, Eve," the bartender said, pulling the girl to her feet. "You're not hurt. Come on now. I buy you a drink and you get back to work."

He gathered the girl's clothes and gave them to her, and they left, the girl still sobbing and clutching her clothes.

Meanwhile, sweat beading his forehead and a pained scowl pinching his horsey features, Pacheca crawled into his own trail-worn duds, donned his cartridge belt and sawed-off Winchester, took another hard pull off a whiskey bottle, and snugged his hat on his head.

Staggering, he moved through the open door, slammed it closed, and made his way down the hall toward the stairs, stumbling over his own huge feet and steadying himself with a hand on each wall. Holding his cheek, he made low bellowing sounds, like those made by an enraged bull standing alone in a pasture corner.

After inquiring with a passerby on the street, he found Doc Romer's office and pulled himself up the building's out-side stairs. When Doc Romer answered Pacheca's pounding knock, his eyes widened. "What in the hell . . . who in the hell are you?"

Pacheca staggered through the door, bulling into Romer

and nearly throwing the doctor off his feet. "Pull it, god-damnit," Pacheca raged, cupping his swollen cheek in his hand, sweat soaking his half-white, half-sandy beard, the birthmark even redder than usual. "Pull the damn thing out!"

Both hands clutching the desk behind him, the doctor scowled up at Pacheca. "What?"

"My tooth," the giant bellowed, sounding as though he had a large rock in his mouth. "Pull the damn tooth! Oh, Christ! Pull the damn thing out!"

The doctor's features flattened and his flush abated as he realized the reason for the bizarre stranger's visit. "Toothache, eh?" Romer felt relief. "I see. Sit down. I'll get my knife. No, not in my chair—you'll break it. Sit on the floor against the wall."

Pacheca obeyed without hesitation, dropping clumsily to his knees, then twisting around on his butt, shoving his back against the wall beside the door.

The doctor reentered the room, carrying a knife and a thin pliers. "I'd offer you more whiskey, but from the smell, I'd say you've had enough."

Pacheca shook his head. "No whiskey. Just cut the sumbitch out . . . *now!*"

"Hold on, hold on," the doctor muttered, moving a green-gold lamp from his desk to the small, round table near Pacheca.

When he'd got it lit, he jerked up his pants at the thighs and dropped to his knees.

"Open wide." He peered inside the big, dark hole of Pacheca's mouth, squinting against the hot, fetid breath. "Wider."

The giant let out a weak groan as he opened his mouth another inch. The doctor canted his own head sideways, squinting into the smelly chasm, looking for the problematic tooth. It wasn't easy to find. They all looked problematic—rotten and crooked and half dead. He'd seen better teeth on taffy-chewing Welsh miners.

"Ah," he said finally. "There we go. Mercy."

He reached inside Pacheca's mouth with the pliers in his right hand, the scalpel in his left. As he tugged and probed, Pacheca pressed the back of his head against the wall, squeezing his eyes closed, cheeks rolled up into his eye sockets.

"Kuuuu," he gargled. "Kuuuu . . . ah . . . gaw . . .ammm-mmm."

"Good Lord," the doctor exclaimed after several minutes, withdrawing his tools and shaking his head with a sigh. "The damn roots must be wrapped around your jaw."

"Oh, for the love o' Job!" Pacheca grabbed the pliers out of the doctor's hand, stuck them into his mouth, closed them over the tooth.

As his hand twisted and pulled, sweat washed over his pale, mottled face. His eyes turned dark and flinty, glazing, the pupils narrowing. A steady groan peeled up from deep in his chest, gradually rising not in volume but in pitch.

Wide-eyed with horror, the doctor backed against his desk.

"Ahhhh!" Pacheca cried at last, his head smacking the wall as his hand jerked back, the pliers exiting his mouth in a spray of blood. In their grip rested the molar, the size of a large-caliber bullet, its snakelike roots dripping thick red drops onto the knotted pine floor.

Pacheca leaned forward and spit a wad into the doctor's basin. Looking up, he saw the doctor staring at him in shock. He removed the tooth from the pliers, slapped it into Romer's hand.

"There you go. Did your job for ye." Pacheca smiled bloodily.

Romer looked up from the tooth in his hand, gray mustache twitching, brown eyes dark with awe. "My God, man. Who are you, anyway?"

"Ruben Pacheca. I'll take that whiskey now."

The doctor eyed him darkly, then climbed to his feet, holding the tooth like something dropped from another planet. He disappeared into the adjacent room, returned without the tooth but with a thick wad of gauze in one hand

and a whiskey bottle in the other. Popping the cork, he handed the bottle to Pacheca still sitting against the wall, spitting blood into the basin.

Pacheca grabbed the bottle, tipped it back, washed the whiskey around in his mouth, then spit it into the basin.

"Pacheca," Romer said thoughtfully, squinting down at the giant. "I've heard of you. Bounty hunter, ain't you?"

Shrugging one shoulder, Pacheca took another deep sip, swirled the whiskey between his cheeks, and swallowed.

"You wouldn't be after Cuno Massey, would you?" the doctor asked him with a knowing twinkle in his left eye.

Pacheca lifted his head sharply, regarding Romer with interest.

The doctor smiled and nodded. "Thought so."

"You seen Massey?" Pacheca asked, eyes kindling.

The building, savage fire in the giant's eyes sent a chill down Romer's spine, and the doctor lost his tongue. As Pacheca climbed slowly to his feet, using the wall to steady himself, Romer stumbled backward, his eyes rising with Pacheca's, until he stared up at the giant from beneath his eyebrows, head tipped back to his shoulders. He was a good foot and a half shorter than his visitor.

"Answer me, you son of a bitch," Pacheca growled, his right fist slowly grabbing a handful of the doctor's collar. "You seen Massey in town?"

The doctor's mustache twitched again, and so did his eyes. He tried to twist loose of the giant's grip, but quickly realized he might as well try to escape the grip of a silver-tipped grizzly.

He cleared his throat and tried to speak, but the giant's grip had pinched his vocal cords. He settled for a nod, eyes bright with fear.

"Where?"

Romer grabbed the giant's fist with both his own, pushed down, trying to loosen the grip. "Let me . . . let me go and I'll tell you," he raked out.

Pacheca released the collar, and Romer sucked a deep draught of air, the deep flush in his face slowly receding.

When he'd taken one more breath, his chest rising and falling, he said, "Three days ago, he came to me with arrow wounds. Kiowa."

Pacheca's voice was low but sharp with vehemence, his eyes bright but hard as granite. "Where'd he go?"

Romer swallowed again, cleared his injured throat. "Left town, northeast. I sent three men after him. They're still after him, far as I know. We were gonna split the reward, but it don't look like my boys are gonna find him. They're miners, not man-trackers."

He swallowed, winced against the ache in his bruised Adam's apple, and shook his head. "He's all yours, far as I'm concerned. Good luck finding him."

Pacheca stared hard at the doctor for a good minute, breathing evenly, his chest rising and falling, his eyes bouncing around in their sockets like billiard balls in tight pockets.

He wasn't seeing the doctor, Romer knew. He was pondering his quarry.

Romer was glad he was no longer Pacheca's quarry.

Finally, the bounty hunter grabbed the gauze out of the doctor's hand, stuffed it into his mouth, packed it tightly over his jaw.

"Thanks," he grunted around the gauze, and marched to the door.

17

MARLENE HAD BEEN right. Cuno needed more rest than he'd thought. He slept most of the first day he'd awakened in the cabin, most of the next day, and even the day after that. He got up only to relieve himself and to see that he wasn't yet ready to walk fifty feet, much less mount a horse.

Slowly, he regained his appetite and was able to eat more and more of Marlene's stews and soups consisting of beans and venison seasoned with herbs, wild onions, and dry rose hips. She brewed a nourishing, aromatic tea from horehound bark she'd found while hunting.

In the afternoon of the third day, Cuno lay awake and alone in the cabin, brooding over the time he was wasting. If it hadn't been for the Kiowas, he would have been halfway to Julesburg by now.

The cabin door opened. Marlene walked in and closed the door behind her, testing the latch. Turning to him, she removed her hat, shook out her hair, letting it fall across her slender shoulders, and tossed the hat on the table. She favored Cuno with a smoky grin.

Cuno pushed up on his elbows. "What the hell are you up to?"

"The shavetail's off checking the traplines."

The devilish smile in place, she unbuttoned her green-plaid shirt.

Her blue eyes slanted like those of some Nordic priestess, a bewitching vixen with the uncanny ability to turn men's hearts to whale blubber. Cuno watched her fingers move down the shirt, laying more and more of her torso bare.

She wasn't wearing her customary undershirt, and as she stripped the wool shirt down her arms and dropped it to the floor, her bare breasts jutted at him, creamy and pink-tipped and bouncing slightly as she moved to unbutton her jeans.

"This supposed to help my leg heal?" Cuno asked, tossing aside his blankets, his pulse racing. This flaxen-haired outlaw vixen cast a mighty powerful spell.

Her voice was husky. "Best medicine I know." She sat down on the cot, kicked off her boots, and removed her jeans and underwear. Meanwhile, Cuno stroked her breasts, outlining the creamy orbs with his fingers, gently pinching her nipples.

Naked, she turned and straddled him, bent over him, allowing him to take her left nipple into his mouth. He ran his hands down her sides until goose pimples rippled her arms and shoulders and the small nipples jutted from her breasts.

She gave a shudder, swallowed, sighed sweetly. Then she spread her thighs further, pushed up on her knees, and helped him enter.

"Feel better already," he breathed as she lowered her head, closed her mouth over his, and began to gently bounce upon him, making the cot creak.

Later they lay naked and entwined, dozing in the afternoon sunshine slanting through a window, hearing a mourning dove's dirge in the middle distance. When he woke, he saw her leaning her head on an elbow, smiling at him.

Without saying a word, she slid her hand up his naked thigh, found him, grasped him gently, caressingly, her slanted Nordic-witch eyes glittering as they burrowed into his. Her lips widened as her smile broadened, and he quickly filled her hand.

She moved to climb back atop him.

"Uh-uh," he said, pushing gently back on her naked shoulder, lifting up on his other arm. "My turn."

"You strong enough?"

He chuckled dryly. "Watch me."

The next day, he was on his feet for several hours, repairing trail gear and currying Renegade and the Arabian. The day after, he spent three hours helping Marlene and Sandy stake and stretch their beaver and fox hides and add them to the plew bales they intended to trade for trail goods when they came to a settlement.

He was fit enough to ride the next day.

After supper, he was drying venison for jerky on a lariat line strung across the cabin. He turned to Marlene, sitting on a bunk and darning a shirt.

"You hear something?" he asked.

She looked up, listening. "No."

Sandy was sitting on the floor near the stove, flipping through a yellowed magazine he'd found in a wood pile behind the cabin. He'd lifted his chin toward the rafters. "Horse."

As if on cue, a whinny rose on the night breezes.

Instantly, Cuno's Colt was in his hand. Heading for the door, he said, "You two stay down."

He cracked the door, peered out. Seeing little but shadows and branches nodding in the breeze, he slipped quickly outside, pressed his back to the cabin, and drew the door until the latch caught.

Squeezing the pistol in his right hand, he listened. Finally, he stepped out into the clearing before the cabin, looked around, and strolled back to where the horses were tied to their picket line.

All stood tensely, ears pricked. Renegade gazed off

across the clearing before the cabin, as if he heard something from that direction.

"What is it, boy?" Cuno stroked his neck and followed his gaze with his own.

He saw nothing but shadows sliding amidst the darkness. Above, bands of stars swathed the velvet sky.

Finally deciding the horses might have heard a raccoon or some other night creature, Cuno headed back to the cabin. If a predator approached, the horses would let him know.

"Anything?" Marlene asked as he stepped inside.

"Nothing, far as I can tell. We best turn in. We'll leave at first light."

He and Sandy undressed and turned into their blankets. When the light was out, Marlene shed her own duds. Only a few minutes passed before she and Sandy were asleep, breathing deeply.

Cuno, however, lay awake on his bunk, arms crossed behind his head. The breeze made the cabin creak. It funneled down the flue and sucked at the ebbing fire. A coyote yapped in the far distance, its song so garbled by the wind it could barely be heard.

Those were the only sounds. Still, Cuno could not relax. A vague unease pricked at the edges of his consciousness, keeping his ears alert, straining, expectant.

Finally, he got up and dressed quietly, securing the Colt around his waist. He was moving toward the door, squinting into the darkness, when he stopped in his tracks.

He'd heard a footfall just outside the door.

The door burst open. It sounded like an explosion in the quiet room. It was still resounding as Cuno dropped to one knee, clawing the Colt from his hip and firing two rounds into the gun flash before him. The attacker's reports combined with his own to make the room sound like the inside of a mine shaft imploded with dynamite.

A slug whistled so close to his head it parted his hair before burying itself in the wall behind him.

A man groaned. In the open doorway, a shadow moved, and a thud followed.

"What the hell's goin' on?" Sandy shouted.

"Stay down!" Cuno yelled, running to the door.

The bearded, barrel-chested man he'd shot lay sprawled on his back in the yard. The man wore heavy canvas trousers and the short-heeled boots favored by miners. The two holes in his chest, spaced a nickel's width apart, gleamed wetly in the starlight. An old-model Navy Colt lay nearby in the grass.

Cuno lifted his gaze. He'd thought he'd seen two shadows in the doorway, and now he was sure of it. A man was skirting the clearing to Cuno's left, not far from the tethered horses.

Cuno ran toward him. It was a halting, clumsy run on his bum leg. Dragging the leg, gritting his teeth against the old pain, he figured he was moving only half as fast as his quarry.

The man disappeared quickly, and when Cuno entered the trees, he stopped. Something moved ahead and to his right. Instinctively, he threw himself left.

Three flashes followed close on the heels of three quick gun reports. Cuno lifted his head to see two large silhouettes burst through the trees, heading away from him. Hooves pounded the leaf-littered ground, bridle chains jangled, and a horse whinnied. It whinnied again as the men galloped away, the sound of thrashing brush and cracking branches diminishing behind them.

Cuno climbed gingerly to his feet and cursed.

Footfalls sounded behind him. He turned and started back toward the cabin, meeting Marlene halfway, her slender figure clad in jeans and an undershirt, rifle in her hands.

She was out of breath. "You okay?"

Cuno nodded. "There were two more. One must have been staying with their horses. They're gone."

"Shit, I thought I covered our trail."

"The doctor's henchmen were bound to find us eventually. We should have been out of here days ago."

"You couldn't ride."

"I can ride now. Let's break camp and vamoose before any more miners decide to try their hand at bounty hunting."

The next day around noon, Ruben Pacheca followed a meandering creek through a narrow valley clotted with pines. Blue jays and magpies chattered in the branches, and a beaver waddled across his trail. The cool air was fragrant with pine needles and fresh snowmelt. But Pacheca wasn't enjoying the scenery.

His jaw ached like hell.

He didn't normally imbibe while tracking, but the whiskey was the only thing that kept the pain down enough that he could ride. The problem was the whiskey made him so drunk he wasn't always sure where he was riding.

Blinking his eyes and sagging back in his saddle, his purple cheek swollen with gauze, he followed a sharp curve in the trail. Suddenly, he stiffened and reined in the big buckskin.

His nostrils flared as he sniffed the breeze. Amidst all the nature smells, coffee.

"I'll be damned." It was just what he needed.

Deciding the smell was coming from straight ahead, he gigged the buckskin forward, concentrating on keeping his eyes focused, biting down hard on the bloody gauze in his jaw. He'd ridden thirty yards when he saw the smoke curling up on the right side of the trail. It was a small fire upon which a black percolator sat. Two men sat cross-legged on either side of the fire while two horses, tied to aspens, cropped grass behind them.

Both men were bearded, hard-looking men in plaid shirts and canvas pants. One appeared old, with a generous sprinkling of salt in his sandy beard. The other man, red-bearded, appeared in his late twenties. The front brim of his shabby hat was pinned to the crown.

"Hello the camp," Pacheca drawled. "I'm comin' in."

As the buckskin pushed through the branches, the

young miner climbed to his feet, one hand on the butt of his rusty Colt Army, the barrel of which protruded a good three inches below his smooth-worn holster made for a smaller gun.

"Easy, Steve," the older man said, regarding Pacheca warily as the big man rode through the trees and halted just beyond the fire.

"Yeah, easy, Steve." Pacheca climbed out of his saddle, losing his grip on the horn and hitting the ground hard on both feet. "I ain't lookin' for trouble," he said, rummaging in his saddlebags for a tin cup, then turning toward the fire. "Just want some o' your mud, that's all."

"Help yourself, pilgrim," the older man said, his tone half-jovial, half-wry as Pacheca, not waiting for the invitation, grabbed the pot off the fire without benefit of the leather scrap lying nearby for that purpose.

The bounty hunter hissed and grunted as he set the pot aside, rubbed his hands on his denims, then again picked up the pot and quickly poured his cup to overflowing.

"Easy there, pilgrim," the younger man said. "Coffee don't grow on trees, you know."

Pacheca took several loud sips of the coffee, slitting his eyes against the steam, acquiring the countenance of a dog who'd just dug up a favorite bone. The deep lines in his massive, drawn face planed out. The birthmark faded slowly to its normal russet.

"Ahhhh," the giant growled, smacking his lips, tilting his head to keep the hot coffee from the bad side of his mouth. "That's good. . . ."

He sat back, resting against a log, his long legs bent before him, both hands on the steaming cup.

Suddenly he frowned, dug around in his mouth with the thumb and index finger of his right hand, plucked out the bloody gauze, and tossed it into the fire. The gauze sizzled and curled, the blood bubbling as it fried, sending up black smoke.

"Heavens to Christ!" the young miner complained. He'd

stooped to grab the coffeepot. Now he recoiled, making a face. "What'd you have to do that for? Ah, Jesus, that stinks!"

Ignoring the man the same way a horse will ignore a stranger talking to it while it eats, Pacheca sipped his coffee, canting his head at the odd angle, muscles jumping in his cheek whenever the hot brew got too close to the crater in his jaw.

Cursing under his breath, the young man leaned forward again, plucked the coffeepot from the fire with the leather wedge, and sloshed its contents.

"Damn near gone," he groused to the older man, who sat regarding Pacheca with keen, wry interest.

"You've had enough, anyway, Steven me boy," the older man said with a faint Irish accent. He didn't take his eyes from Pacheca. "We best get back trailin' again soon."

Steven poured the last of the coffee into his cup—a half cup's worth—and sat back against a rock, shuttling his surly gaze to the stranger. "Who the hell are you, anyways?"

Pacheca rolled his big, watery eyes up and over to the lad. He stared hard at him for several seconds. As if the stare wasn't answer enough, he said, "I knew a young man, not much younger than you, that got his nose cut off for pokin' it around where it didn't belong."

The young man stared back, unfazed by the threat. "What happened to your jaw?"

"Easy, Steven," the older man said, smiling. "Our friend here is the great Ruben Pacheca." The smile lifted his gray beard, made his hazel eyes dance. "Bounty hunter—famous in these parts. *In*-famous, I should say."

Pacheca shuttled his eyes to the older man. His gaze was black, expressionless. He sipped his coffee.

"You're after Cuno Massey, eh, Pacheca?"

The bounty hunter wrinkled a nostril and growled evenly. "I take it you're after him, your ownselves."

Steven tossed his curious gaze from Pacheca to the older man. "How in the hell did he know that?"

The older man answered for Pacheca, who remained silent, cup held to his mouth like a communion chalice.

"Why else would two rock farmers be out here with guns instead of picks?"

Ignoring the man, Pacheca nodded at the corked bottle resting beside him. "Give me a shot o' your whiskey."

Steven grunted with exasperation. "Anything else?"

"The whiskey'll do."

"Make him pay for it, Hugh."

Hugh picked up the bottle, his wry, cunning smile in place. "Where's your trail manners, Steven? Haven't I taught you anything?"

He handed the bottle across the fire to Pacheca, who uncorked it and took a big sip. He sloshed the whiskey around in his mouth, tipped his head back, and swallowed. Sighing with pleasure, he dumped several jiggers in his coffee, then corked the bottle, and tossed it back to Hugh.

"Obliged," he mumbled under his breath.

"Looks like you need it worse than we do," Hugh said. He tossed the bottle back to Pacheca, who caught it against his chest.

Pushing up from his knees, Hugh said, "Well, laddie, what do you say we head on up the trail?"

Staring at the fire, Pacheca formed a taut smile. "Wouldn't do that if I was you."

"Wouldn't do what?" Steven asked wearily.

"Tangle with Cuno Massey. He takes to killin' the way a pig takes to warm mud."

"We can take him. Just you—"

"Easy, Steve," Hugh interrupted. "Our friend Pacheca's probably right. We found out last night that Massey's wily as a wolverine, but for five thousand dollars, I reckon we gotta try."

Pacheca chuckled, sipping his whiskey-laced coffee, and chased it with a swig from the bottle. "Yeah, you'll try. I'll be right behind you . . . to mop up the blood." He chuckled again and shook his head.

Flushed with anger, Steve jutted his chin at him, but Hugh grabbed his shoulder, silencing the younger man. "Come on, Steve. Grab your coffeepot. We're burnin' sunlight."

"There ye go," Pacheca said. "You're burnin' daylight."

"Good day to ye, sir," Hugh told the bounty hunter with a sly wink. "Nice meetin' ye, so to speak."

When the two would-be bounty hunters had tightened their saddle cinches, they forked leather and rode off through the trees, cantering west along the trail hugging the stream. When the sounds of their footfalls had faded, replaced by chirping birds and the gurgling water, Pacheca yawned and sat back against the log, stretching his legs and crossing his ankles.

The coffee hadn't perked him up. The whiskey had numbed his jaw, but it was also drawing his eyelids closed. He drained the bottle, threw it aside. Ah, well, he'd take a little snooze—fifteen minutes or so. . . .

He woke later, jerking his head up, blinking the sleep from his eyes and looking around. The fire was nothing but gray ash. Not even a tendril of smoke lifted from the stone ring.

The sun angled westward. Damn. He must have slept a couple of hours, at least.

His heart pulled with alarm, and he turned quickly. His horse was not where he'd left it, ground-tied only a few feet away.

He pushed himself to his feet, staring westward along the creek, as though if he looked hard enough he would still see the two miners leading his horse away. But they'd probably snuck back and grabbed the buckskin, stranding him afoot, only a few minutes after he'd nodded off.

That meant they had a couple of hours on him. And that gap would do nothing but grow.

Anger searing his veins and swelling his heart, Pacheca bunched his trembling fists, threw his head back, and roared.

18

HUGH AND STEVE followed the stream through the wooded ravine for five miles. They halted their horses at dusk and dismounted.

Hugh walked a ways down the canyon. When he returned, he and the younger Steven waited along the stream as the sun plunged behind the western ridges, filling the canyon with cool darkness and night sounds.

They built no fire. They ate only the hardtack they'd had in their saddlebags when they'd been summoned by the doctor.

"You sure they're up there?" Steven asked, pinching his beard and gazing eastward down the canyon.

"They're up there."

"How do you know it ain't fur trappers you saw?"

"I got eyes, me boy. Even an old man like me."

"So when we gonna take him?"

"When I say and not a minute sooner."

"What are we gonna do about the kid and the girl?"

"Kill 'em."

Steven looked at Hugh.

Hugh shrugged. "It's the safest way. They all have guns, don't they?"

Steven directed his wide, thoughtful eyes back down the canyon, where the water gurgled over boulders and the last day birds sang, flitting their shadows against the violet sky. "Yeah, they gotta be vermin, anyway—runnin' with the likes of Massey."

They waited on the rocks. Hugh nibbled hardtack. Steven just stared off down the canyon.

When the stars were brilliant overhead, Hugh said, "Okay." He stood, picked up his Spencer carbine, patted the old five-shot Remington in his sagging holster, and began walking along the stream. "Follow me. Watch your step and don't make any noise."

"Don't talk to me like I'm some damn tinhorn."

"You are some damn tinhorn. Now shut up!"

Quietly, they made their way along the stream, stepping over driftwood, bringing their feet down softly in the deep buffalo and grama grass. When they came to a right-angling bend in the stream, they stopped at the edge of an aspen grove.

"Quietly now," Hugh whispered in Steven's ear. "Ever so quietly."

The older man took his rifle in both arms and moved slowly, one step at a time, through the trees. Steven followed directly behind him, holding his big Colt Army in his left hand.

His heart pounded. He breathed through his mouth to make as little noise as possible. His hand was slick against the revolver's scarred stock. He took the gun in his right hand, wiped the left against his thigh, then replaced the gun in his left hand and continued walking quietly through the trees, avoiding branches.

The umber glow of a low fire grew before him. Besides the stars, it was the only light. It made the darkness around Hugh and Steven seem even darker.

As they approached the fire, Hugh gestured for Steven

to move off to the right. Hugh moved to the left of the fire, closing on it in a gradual arc.

When the men came to within twenty feet of the fire and the tack scattered here and there about rocks, pine saplings, and fallen logs, they stopped. Hugh stared ahead, smiling grimly.

Three blanket rolls lay humped about the fire, each capped with a downward-tilted hat. A coffeepot gurgled weakly on a rock in the fire's small ring. Two rifles leaned against rocks.

Shit, this is gonna be easy, Steven thought. His heart lightened. He raised his old hogleg and thumbed the hammer back.

He was about to take aim when he heard old Hugh growl, "Shit!"

Steven turned to him. Hugh stared at the encampment, his eyes wide, his face creased with alarm. Confounded, Steven followed the older man's gaze, squinting.

Then he saw what Hugh saw. The bundles were too neat, each hat too perfectly positioned. It was a setup.

The thought had just blazed a hot path through his brain when the sound of three gun hammers being pulled back ratcheted across the night. A twig snapped under a boot directly behind him.

"You two really shoulda stayed with your sluice boxes," a man's voice said somewhere behind and between Steven and Old Hugh.

There's was a long, deafening silence. Steven's heart pummeled his rib cage.

"Don't do it, Hugh," he said to himself, reading Hugh's mind. "If you do it, I'm gonna have to."

An eye wink later, Hugh gave a bellow as he whipped around, his six-gun blazing. Automatically, Steven turned then, too, raising his own hogleg.

All he heard before he died, bullets tunneling through him as he floated back on a soft cushion of air, was the caterwaul of a sudden storm.

•   •   •

Cuno, Marlene, and Sandy left the two would-be bush-whackers where they lay, and headed east out of the mountains.

Two days later they stopped at a trading post on the outskirts of Colorado Springs, where they traded the Arabian and their plews for several sacks of Pride of Denver flour, coffee, beans, sugar, salt, bacon, medicinal whiskey, and ammunition.

Cuno had stayed in the mountains for as long as possible, believing he was safer there than on the plains. The long, hot, dusty ride across Colorado's eastern desert proved him wrong. The only trouble they ran into was six Pawnee bucks, who followed them distantly for two days before attempting a halfhearted attack on the north bank of Hell Creek. When it came down to it, the bucks had no stomach for fighting, and were easily discouraged when Cuno, Sandy, and Marlene emptied a cylinder each in their direction.

After two weeks in the greasewood and sage, skirting low, crumbling mesas and fording one dry creek bed after another, they crossed the Overland Stage road connecting Julesburg and Denver. Avoiding the road, which would have been a faster route than their cross-country game and Indian trails, but more populated and dangerous, they continued east to the South Fork of the Republican River. They followed the wide, muddy stream northeast for a day, then headed due north, picking up the South Fork of the Platte two days later.

It was late August when they topped a sage-tufted knoll and reined their horses to a halt, squinting against the sun and their own dust catching up to them. Below lay the town on the south side of the South Platte River, where the trouble had begun when Cuno had killed Vince Evans on the third floor of Roderick's Hotel.

It was a bitter homecoming. As Cuno stared down at the dusty, swaybacked town of false-fronted businesses and mud and adobe dwellings carved from the sage and grease-wood, bile boiled in his guts.

He was close now, so very close to the man who'd put the bounty on his head, caused the death of his beloved July, and made his life a living hell.

"What now?" Marlene asked, voicing his thoughts.

Cuno spit a weed stem from his mouth and gigged Renegade down the knoll. "Come on. I know where we can hole up for a few days, until I can figure it all out."

They rode over to the main trail and followed it into town. Julesburg was on the busy Overland Trail, and as they threaded their way past the tattered Civil War Army tents and slab-sided sheds on the town's outskirts, they had to thread their way through the bull and mule trains, as well.

Mule skinners and bull-whackers bellowed and cracked blacksnakes over the lathered teams. Dry wheels squawked for grease. In the creaking, swaying Conestogas, in the platform-spring drays and heavy-duty farm wagons equpped with chains from axle to doubletree for sharp cornering, kids yelled and babies bawled. Sun-seared women and girls sat the high seats beside men looking worn-out and ornery, fore-arms bulging as they manipulated the leather ribbons in their bony fists.

The scouts and outriders, clad in dusty trail garb and mounted on muscular pintos and quarter horses, wasted lit-tle time in heading for Julesburg's many watering holes. It was only a little after noon, but the hitch racks before the sun-baked cantinas were jammed, and pianos clanged like they normally did after dark.

Roderick's Hotel was the only mansard-roofed, three-story building in town. Cuno was glad to see it still stand-ing. On the savage frontier, businesses and structures didn't last much longer than the men who ran or built them.

Keeping his hat pulled low over his forehead, Cuno made his way through the brush behind the buildings lining the north side of the main avenue. Hogs and chickens for-aged back there—some penned, some not—and Cuno led

Marlene and Sandy through them to the back of Roderick's Hotel.

A staircase of white, chipped paint ran up the rear, with landings and doors on both the second and third floors. At ground level, under the second-floor landing, another door opened into what Cuno remembered as a storage room.

"Sandy, this is gonna be up to you."

The boy turned his sun-seasoned face to Cuno, a pale streak just above his eyes where the hat shielded him from the sun. "What's that?"

"I want you to walk around and enter the hotel through the front. Inside, you'll probably see a thin old man sitting behind a desk. Tell him you have a message for a girl named Glory. If—"

"Who's Glory?" Marlene asked, giving Cuno a lopsided frown.

Ignoring her, Cuno kept his eyes on Sandy. "If Glory isn't there, give the message to Frieda. If Frieda isn't there—"

"Who's Frieda?" Marlene interrupted again, her frown digging deeper into her forehead, her voice growing sharper, more indignant.

Cuno shushed her quickly and turned back to Sandy, continuing. "Give the message to Minnie."

Marlene folded her arms across her chest and pouted. *"Who in the hell is Minnie?"*

"You'll find out soon . . . I hope."

"What am I supposed to tell her?" Sandy asked.

"Tell her she has an old friend who wants to talk to her outside, behind the sty back there. Give her the message personally. If the old man's nosy, tell him it's business. He should understand."

"Can I tell 'em your name?"

"No. The girl might repeat it out loud. Go."

Eager to please, Sandy slipped out of his saddle, tossed his reins up to Cuno, and walked quickly around the building, scattering several wyandottes pecking through kitchen refuse. Meanwhile, Cuno and Marlene gigged their horses behind the horse stable with a lean-to pigsty in which several sows rooted and grunted and knocked the cracked wood planks topped with barbed wire.

"They'll think it's business?" Marlene groused at him. "Whores, I take it." Her tone was rife with jealousy.

Cuno had dismounted and was peering around the sty at the hotel. "Those whores saved my life. I hate like hell involving them, but I see no other way."

"A whorehouse is no place for a boy. You should have sent me."

"The girls have only the third floor. The rest of the place is a bona-fide hotel." Cuno allowed himself a smile. "Besides, if I'd sent you, I'd probably have a she-fight on my hands."

Making a sour face as she sat her horse, Marlene turned away. "Are they . . . pretty?" she asked after several seconds.

Cuno smiled again, facing the hotel, but decided to forgo an answer. Circumstances, he realized of a sudden, had sent him into some of the trickiest territory he'd yet negotiated.

19

CUNO AND MARLENE waited behind the pig-
pen in testy silence. Sandy appeared about ten minutes after he'd entered the hotel. He strolled, whistling casually,
along the worn path from the main avenue. Looking around
and seeing no one, he broke into a run that brought him
back behind the pigsty.

"Well?" Cuno asked.

"I found Miss Glory. She was takin' a bath." A faint
flush rose under the boy's sunburned cheeks. "She didn't
sound very thrilled, but she said since it's been slow lately
she'd come." The flush rose higher in his face, deepening.

"So, it's been slow lately, huh?" Marlene said snidely to
Cuno, who shrugged.

A quarter hour must have passed before the sound of a
door closing rose to Cuno's ears. He looked around the sty.
A short girl appeared wearing a bed robe over a powder-
blue nightgown. Her long blond hair hung wet around
her shoulders, water droplets glistening. Frowning, she
glanced at the sky, blinking her eyes against the bright sun,
then opened a parasol and walked across the lot toward the
pigpen.

"Behind the sty, my eye," she groused loudly enough for Cuno to hear.

As she approached, she saw him standing at the corner of the tawdry structure, and stopped, planting an angry fist on a hip and looking up at him, pinching her petal-mouthed, unpainted doll's face angrily. "Look here, *friend,* I don't know who you think you are, but—"

Cuno lifted his head, smiling as he poked his hat brim back.

"Oh, my goodness gracious," Glory exclaimed under her breath, her pale, round face going whiter. "Cuno Massey—*you're alive!*"

She dropped her parasol and threw her arms around his neck, burying her face in his chest. "I thought for sure, after all these months, with all those wanted dodgers old Evans sent out . . ."

"Yeah, I did, too," Cuno said, peeling her arms from his neck and stooping to gaze directly into her face. "Listen, can you hole us up for a while?" He looked around to indicate Sandy and Marlene, who stood a few feet away, hip cocked, arms crossed on her chest, regarding Glory with unadulterated scorn.

"Sure," Glory said, squinting her eyes with incredulity while squeezing his arm with alarm, "but, Cuno, what are you doing in Julesburg?"

"I gotta score to settle, Glory. You know who with. If you don't want me around the hotel, I'll understand, but I'd appreciate it if you'd put up Marlene and Sandy for a few days."

"After what you did for us—drillin' some daylight through that bastard woman-beater Vince Evans?" Glory paused and pinched Sandy's hat brim. "Pardon my French, sonny."

Regarding Cuno again: "Don't be silly. Our home is yours for as long as you need it . . . but I can't say that's gonna be long if you're going after Franklin Evans."

"Thanks, Glory. We'll stable our horses down the street, where old Roderick won't see them, and be right back."

Cuno, Marlene, and Sandy stabled their horses at the
South Platte Livery and Feed Barn, then climbed the outside stairs at the rear of Roderick's Hotel, slumped under
the weight of their saddlebags and rifles. Waiting for them,
Glory opened the door and led them down a narrow, dim
hall, the walls papered in gilded red flower patterns.

"You can have my room," Glory said. "I'll sleep in
Frieda's room."

"Sleep, I'm sure," Marlene grunted sarcastically behind
Cuno, who ignored her.

They were halfway down the hall when a door opened
ahead. A short, swarthy cowboy emerged, a quirley in his
lips, a sheepish smile curling his thick, black mustache. As
he stepped into the hall, he slicked his hair back with one
hand and set an overlarge, Dakota-creased hat on his head.

"Don't make yourself a stranger now, Charlie," a girl
called from the room. As she moved toward the door, her
shadow grew in the hall.

Cuno lowered his head as the cowboy passed, then
raised it again. Before him, in the open doorway, stood a
chubby girl with rich auburn hair hanging straight down
her back to her waist. Clad in gossamer silk and smoking a
cigarette in a long, wooden holder, she owned the round,
dark-eyed face of a Slav. Her breasts were deep and pear-
shaped behind the sheer fabric, the large nipples canted
outward. Cuno smiled, and the girl frowned up at him,
thoughtful.

"Hi, Frieda."

The girl's frown etched itself deeper, her dark doe's
eyes flashing gold. "Cuno?" She blinked her eyes and removed the cigarette holder from her thin but sensuous
mouth. "Cuno Massey?" She took two steps toward him.
"What on earth are you doing in Julesburg—are you
crazy?"

"I reckon," Cuno said. "We'll be stayin' here a while—
if you and Minnie don't mind, that is. This here is Marlene.
The whip is Sandy. Friends of mine."

"Hi, Sandy," Frieda said with a smile, which lost a

touch of its luster as she turned to Marlene. To Cuno, she said, "What'd you do, get yourself hitched?"

"I've kept my head above water so far," Cuno said with a wry glance at Marlene.

Marlene shook the hand and said cattily, "That's quite an outfit you have there. Sandy, avert your eyes."

"Thanks, I'm thrilled you like it," Frieda said coolly, giving her eyes a slow blink as she turned her gaze again to Cuno. "We all owe you a favor—especially Minnie. She'd be pushing up prickly pears on boot hill if you hadn't done away with that Evans trash. But I'll ask again, what are you doing here?"

"I'm here to get a bounty off my head."

Frieda turned to Glory, who shrugged. Turning back to Cuno, Frieda shook her head gravely. "That's crazy. I'm impressed you're still alive, with that bounty on your head, but Cuno, you don't have a chance against Evans's Muleshoe crew. Not a whore's chance at the Pearly Gates. Sorry, Sandy," she added with a nod to the boy, who was too busy staring in a catatonic daze at her bountiful tits.

"Thanks for the note of confidence, Frieda," Cuno raked out with a wry smile.

"Cuno," Frieda said, stepping up close to him and grabbing his shell belt, giving him a schoolmarm's jerk, "don't be crazy. Leave here. Go to Canada. Go to Mexico. You're still alive. That means you're ahead of the game."

"Just forget about the bounty on my head?"

"Yes," another voice said.

Cuno turned as a door opened across the hall. Another girl appeared—a brown-eyed, tawny-haired young woman with a tomboy's figure similar to Marlene's. Her face was narrow, with a fine nose, pointed chin, and heavy-lidded eyes. Her hair hung straight to her shoulders, falling from a man's funnel-brimmed hat. She wore a man's overlarge, pin-striped shirt with the oversized sleeves rolled up her arms. The shirt was nearly all she wore. Her long, slender but shapely legs were naked except for the high-topped, stovepipe boots with cavalry spurs.

The shirt sagged open, revealing a goodly portion of both high, apple-round breasts.

"What have you brought us to, a damn dairy farm?" Marlene muttered.

"I agree," Minnie said, her voice customarily slow and lazy and gravelly. "Forget about the bounty. Leave here, Cuno."

"Not until I get my life back, and that won't happen until the bounty's gone."

"You don't know what you're getting into."

"Can't be much worse that what I've already been through."

"Yes, it can," Minnie said, her slender face forming a wry smile as she tilted her head slightly.

Cuno looked at Frieda and Glory, both standing with their eyes downcast. An awkward silence pooled.

"What's going on?" Cuno asked Minnie, having the distinct sense there was more to be said. "How do you know so well what Evans is capable of?"

"Oh, don't ask her," Glory breathed, turning away.

Cuno stared at Minnie. She stared back, her eyes acquiring a fine sheen, her smile broadening, until several large tears spilled down her cheeks.

Turning slowly, she wriggled her shoulders. The shirt fell down her arms, baring her back. Behind him, Marlene gasped. Long, white welts were etched across Minnie's slender back, from her delicate shoulders to her waist, the healed scars chewing, gouging, and knotting the once-flawless, creamy skin. It was like looking at a lovely painting slashed to ribbons with a bowie knife.

There had to be ten lashes, at least, though it was hard to tell for sure. Several overlapped.

The thought of a bullwhip wielded against this tough but tender, vulnerable girl made Cuno's molars grind and his jaws ache.

Sniffing and jerking her head, composing herself, Minnie said, "I do thank you for saving me from Vince." She lifted the shirt and turned to Cuno, her eyes staunch and ironic once again. "But his father isn't much nicer."

Cuno engulfed her in his arms. She stood stiffly, arms at her sides. "I'm sorry."

"God knows it wasn't your fault," she said, her tough old self again. "I was just showin' you how much you don't want to tangle with Evans and his men." She smiled ironically. "It didn't do any good, did it?"

"No, it sure didn't." He smiled back at her. In fact, seeing the scars only cemented his resolve. Franklin Evans would die a hideous death.

He kissed Minnie's forehead, then turned to Glory, who showed him, Marlene, and Sandy to their room. When they'd dumped their saddlebags on the floor, Glory said from the doorway, "I'll send up water for baths. Shall I bring two tubs up, or just one?"

"One," Marlene said. Entwining her hands around Cuno's arm, she gave Glory a catty smile.

Glory returned the smile in kind, and grabbed Sandy's hand. "Come on, sugar," she said. "You can stay with me and Frieda."

Glimpsing Cuno's concerned look, she said, "Oh, don't worry. He's cute, but I'm not craven!" Pulling Sandy into the hall, she closed the door.

Turning, Cuno saw Marlene regarding him skeptically, lovely, slanted eyes slanted more than usual. "Just how well do you know these girls, anyway?"

For the next two days, Cuno lay low, biding his time and considering his options. Sandy and Marlene brought food back to the room. Otherwise, all three of them stayed close to the hotel's third floor, careful that the girls' customers didn't see them.

Whenever Frieda or Glory had a client, Sandy was sent back to Marlene and Cuno's room. He'd ask with a sheepish, knowing grin, "What are they doin' in there, anyway?"

"Playin' dominoes," Cuno would say as he cleaned his gun or laid out a fresh solitaire hand.

Repairing tack or flipping through a magazine, Marlene would snicker.

Late on the third night of their stay at Roderick's, Cuno woke suddenly. The room was dark. The street below the open windows lay silent. A figure moved to his left, and there were the sibilant sounds of someone gathering clothes and dressing.

It was Marlene. When she'd donned a clean shirt and denims, she gently stepped into her boots—slowly, carefully, obviously trying to make as little sound as possible. Cuno's first impulse was to ask her what she was doing, but something held his tongue.

Ever since she had killed the Mexican bounty hunter, he'd harbored vague reservations about her. So vague that most of the time he wasn't even aware of them himself. He hadn't wanted to acknowledge them, because he'd found himself falling in love with the girl.

He had to acknowledge them now, however. It didn't make sense, her getting up and going out in a wide-open town like Julesburg in the middle of the night.

He lay there, feigning sleep, until she quietly opened the door and left the room. When the bolt clicked in the latch, he threw the covers back and reached for his clothes.

20

WHEN CUNO HAD dressed and strapped his gun and cartridge belt around his waist, he left the room and strode quickly down the hall, dark and silent at this late hour. He left the building by the rear door, paused on the landing to scan the night-cloaked lot with its stable and pigpen, then quickly descended the stairs on the balls of his feet.

At the bottom, he hurried around the building to the street, paused again, and looked around. A block away on his right, a saloon was still lit up but quiet, only a handful of hang-headed, hip-shot horses tethered out front. From the stars, Cuno figured it was around three A.M.

The only sounds were the breeze and a lone dog yapping out by the river.

Looking left, Cuno saw a slender, shadowy figure disappear around the land office on the other side of the street. He loped that way, ducking under a hitch rack, mounting the boardwalk, and shouldering up to the building. His hat brushed a low-hanging shingle; he reached up quickly to silence its squawk and edged a look around a corner of the whipsawed shack, looking south toward scattered tents and

shanties and the infinite, star-draped Colorado desert beyond.

Marlene walked away from him, vagrant light reflecting
off her denims, shirt, and hair bobbing down from her hat.
Cuno stepped around the corner, following her through the
soft dirt of the side street, avoiding fresh horse apples. He
walked quickly, squinting, picking her out of the night
shadows.

When she came to a tar-paper shack and corral in which
a dozen oxen milled, heavy-footed and snorting, she angled off the trail, disappearing behind the shack. Cuno
broke into a jog. He sidled up to the shack and stole a
glance behind, where a knoll rose, framed and flanked by
spindly cottonwood trees.

Looking cautiously to either side, making sure no one
else was about, Cuno cat-footed forward through the sage
bushes and dropped to his knees behind the knoll, lifting
his chin and pricking his ears.

He heard Marlene's voice. "No!" she exclaimed in a
raking whisper beyond the knoll. She said more, but Cuno
couldn't discern the words.

A male, Mexican-accented voice replied in angry tones.

A bona fide argument ensued. Cuno could hear only
snippets, which told him generally that Marlene had agreed
to something she was backing out on, piss-burning the
Mexican.

He wasn't just piss-burned, he was threatening.

"Let me go, you son of a sow!" Marlene snapped, loud
and clear, evoking an alarmed moo from an ox behind Cuno.

Adrenaline jetting, Cuno leapt to his feet. As he jogged
around the knoll, the sound of a slap was heard. Marlene
cried out, cursing like a trail cook.

"Hey!" Cuno yelled as he rounded the knoll and peered
through the cottonwoods.

Marlene lay on her butt, pushing up on her elbows. A tall
man with a drooping paunch and high-peaked sombrero
stood over her, reaching for her arm. At Cuno's voice, he

froze and jerked his head up, his right hand slapping the revolver on his hip.

The Mexican's gun was still clearing leather when
Cuno's Colt barked and flashed. The bullet took the man
through his right arm, spinning him around and evoking a
Spanish curse. The man turned back, bringing the gun up
again.

Before he could get off another shot, Cuno's Colt leapt
and clapped twice more, and the man staggered backward,
and dropped to his knees, hands at his sides, the black O of
his mouth trying feebly to form words while the English
Bisley inched up once again.

Cuno shot him through the head, blowing his sombrero
down his back. The Mexican fell backward, squashing it.

Lowering his Colt, Cuno walked over to Marlene, who
stayed down on her elbows, gazing up at him. Her hat lay
several feet away on the ground. Her hair was splashed
across her face and head.

She didn't say anything, just stared up at him, her eyes
guilty, defeated, with a only vague shadow of her customary defiance.

"Spill it," he demanded, standing over her, feet spread,
Colt hanging down by his thigh. His left fist was tightly
clenched at his side, as though ready to strike.

"You ain't gonna like it," she said quietly.

"I have a feelin'."

"That was Pablo Mirado's brother, Raoul," she said.

Cuno's heart burned, threatening to squeeze through
his ribs. He didn't say anything, just waited for her to con-
tinue.

"Pablo was part of our gang," she said. "The morning
we ambushed you, he'd gotten into an argument with
Jess, and he hung back from the group. When he found
the rest of the gang dead, he followed us—you, me, and
Sandy."

"Pablo wasn't going for his gun when you shot him,
was he?"

Marlene shook her head. "I shot him because he was a fool and because I didn't want to share the reward."

"What were you going to do—backshoot me, or stab me some night while I slept?"

"One or the other, most likely. I was going to wait until we were a little closer to Julesburg."

"My destination was nice and convenient for you. No haulin' the body for days in the hot sun. Or were you just going to take my head back to Evans?"

She shrugged a shoulder, dipped her head shamefully. "I hadn't gotten that far yet."

"What's the deal with Raoul?"

"When you were healing in the cabin from the arrow wounds, I rode down to Canyon City one day and wired him in Denver. He'd been part of our gang once, too, only he and Jess parted company a little over a year ago."

Her gaze softened, and she swallowed, shook stray wisps of hair from her eyes. "I couldn't take you down . . . not after we'd made love. I'd let Raoul do it."

"And you'd split the reward."

"Oh, no," she said, gazing off, her tone dull and self-deprecating. "I'd kick Raoul off some night after he'd curled up on the bottom of a whiskey bottle."

Cuno glanced at the dead Mexican. "What happened?"

Her eyes softened even more, and for a moment it appeared she was going to sob. "I reckon somewhere between here and Canyon City—or maybe even before Canyon City—I fell in love with you."

Cuno didn't say anything. Seeing the cold look in his eyes, Marlene climbed to her feet and moved stiffly toward him. She placed her hands on his chest.

"Please, Cuno," she said, a light sheen of emotion glazing her eyes, "I know it sounds bad, but I've changed. I love you. Please, believe me. . . ."

She wrapped her hands around his neck, tried to kiss him, but he tipped his head back and away from her. He took her wrists in his hands, slowly but forcefully pushed her away.

"Fool me once, shame on you," he said tightly, nostrils flaring. "Fool me twice, shame on me."

"Cuno, please—"

"You can clean your things out of the room tomorrow, when I'm not there. Until then, I don't know what you're gonna do, and I can't say as I give a shit."

Stiffly, he turned and walked away.

After a sleepless night, and leaving Sandy in the charge of the three pleasure girls at Roderick's, Cuno was on the trail heading southeast of Julesburg just after sunrise the next day. Having come up with no satisfactory plan in town for dealing with Franklin Evans, he'd decided to ride out to the Evans range and play it by ear.

He entertained a half-baked notion of stealing onto the ranch compound after dark, getting into the house, and somehow isolating Evans from the rest of the household. After the hell Evans had made of Cuno's life, Cuno wanted to give the bastard a slow, painful send-off to the Smoking Gates, but he doubted he'd have time to do much more than simply pink the son of a bitch.

Not and be able to get off the ranch alive, that is.

On the other hand, he didn't really care if he lived or died, as long as Franklin Evans died miserably. He'd found himself unexpectedly falling in love, but that was gone now, too.

Marlene, like virtually everyone else he'd met in the past year, and in spite of her passionate lovemaking, had been out only for the bounty on his head. She'd strung him along like a kitten on a scrap of yarn for too many miles. He wouldn't trust her now as far as he could throw an elephant into a strong wind.

The memory of last night raked his haunches once again, and he lifted his head from the shaggy two-track trail he was following, looking around to distract himself as much as to get his bearings.

At the bottom of a long, easy grade to his right lay a

creek framed by burr oaks, box elders, and willows. To his
left rose a bluff with patches of sage and buffalo grass, its
steep sides pitted, eroded, and cluttered with gravel slides,
its base strewn with boulders. According to the livery hostler
back in Julesburg, the Evans Muleshoe Ranch lay straight
ahead, beyond the creek curving onto the trail ahead of him.

All Cuno could see, however, was an endless expanse of
saffron prairie-desert folding down into shallow cuts and
dry washes and rising abruptly to infrequent buttes and
mesas and short jogs of distant hills. Meadowlarks sang
from rocks and shrubs, and prairie dogs chortled from a
vast expanse of holes and sandy hummocks lying thirty
yards down the grade toward the creek.

Cuno gigged Renegade ahead, crossing the creek and
following the trail for another two miles before approaching a timbered sign arched over the road, the Muleshoe
brand blazed into it. On the right side of the road stood another, smaller sign on a single post. PRIVATE PROPERTY, it
read, KEEP OUT. Below, another board had been added
bearing underlined red letters: THIS MEANS YOU!

Cuno looked around. He was on a table, with no ridges
or trees or other cover for hundreds of yards. Seeing none
of Evans's riders, he gigged Renegade under the arch and
rode a half mile up the trail before branching off cross-
country, heading east through a shallow valley at the bottom
of which twisted a rocky wash. As he rode, he suppressed
the memory of last night with Marlene by working on a
way to slip onto the Muleshoe compound and deal Franklin
Evans some old-fashioned, frontier justice—with as much
mercy as his bounty hunters had shown July.

Cuno's thoughts broke off abruptly when he heard
something on the breeze. Reining Renegade to a halt, he
touched the butt of his Colt and lifted his head, listening.

There it was again—a tinny sound, like water or a distant
wind chime made small by the breeze and distance and the
singing grasshoppers.

Deciding the sound came from over the ridge to his left,
he gigged Renegade that way, climbing the ridge covered

with minty-smelling sage. He halted the horse and looked around. Below lay a deep, narrow valley threaded by another wash and several spindly cottonwoods.

"Help! Someone please help me!"

The woman's voice rose from beyond the next steep ridge.

Cuno glanced around for a route across the deep-scored valley. Riding south several yards, he came to an angling deer trail, followed it down the ridge, through the thick brush and across the narrow, rocky wash at the bottom.

While he rode he heard the woman's intermittent pleas, pinched with desperation but growing louder. By the time he made the base of the opposite ridge, he and Renegade were covered with burrs and pussy-willow seeds. Finding another game trail, Cuno climbed the chalky, eroded slope to the narrow peak, and stared off to the east.

Beyond was a vast expanse of sunbaked badlands—deep-scored canyons separated by rocky scarps and sandstone buttes cut millions of years ago by powerful, glacier-fed streams. In the distance, a great golden eagle traced lazy circles in the brassy sky, this vast devil's obstacle course no doubt a lucrative hunting ground.

"Thank God!" came the woman's cry again, much louder and clearer this time. "Please help me!"

Cuno lowered his eyes. Sixty feet down the steep, rocky slope tufted with hard, dry shrubs and bunchgrass, a young woman stood on a narrow ledge. Her head was tipped back, revealing a pretty, delicate face, round brown eyes staring up at him beseechingly. Thick cinnamon hair blew around in the breeze. She wore a cream blouse with puffy sleeves, a green wool riding skirt, and matching cloth boots with high heels. The blouse and skirt were torn. Blood glistened on her right arm.

"I've been trapped here for two hours," she called up to him. "My horse threw me."

"Hold on," Cuno said, dismounting. He plucked his lariat from the saddle and paid it down the slope. "Can you get it?"

"Got it!" she called back. He watched as she grabbed the rope with both hands but favoring her right arm.

"Wrap it around your waist and tie it."

She wrapped the rope around her waist and lowered her head as she tied the knot. She took a long time.

"What's the matter?" Cuno called finally.

Lifting her head, her lovely face pinched with frustration, she said, "I'm afraid I injured my hand. I can't tie the knot."

"Hold on." He turned Renegade around, facing back down the gentle slope they'd just climbed, away from the girl in the ravine.

"Stay, boy, stay," he ordered the horse, then turned back to the ravine and began crawling down the steep, rocky slope toward the girl, testing each rock and crevice before planting his feet and hands. The descent wasn't difficult until he was ten feet from the bottom, where the hand-and footholds suddenly gave way to a wall of smooth clay.

He paused, looking down.

"Careful," the girl said, her voice trembling slightly.

Cuno looked around for an easy way down. The ledge upon which the girl stood was only about six feet square. The sheer wall extended a good ten feet on either side of it.

"Step to the right as far as you can," Cuno called to her.

When she was hugging the right side of the ledge, Cuno turned and let himself fall straight down, arms thrust out for balance. He hit the left side of the ledge, bounding forward and grinding his feet into the sandstone beneath him before his momentum could carry him over the edge.

The girl reached out and grabbed his arm, pulling him back against the butte. "Oh, God!" she exclaimed as he scrambled forward. "I thought you were going over."

Cuno turned to her, his eyes traveling from her pretty, delicately carved face with full, wide lips and lustrous eyes down her fine, alabaster neck, to her chamise-clad bosom, partly exposed by her soiled blouse from which several buttons were missing. She was tall, slender, and high-breasted, with a dark, heart-shaped mole on her neck. Self-consciously, she pulled the top of the garment closed with her left hand.

"Are you all right?"

"Yes," she said. "Just scratched and bruised. I was riding the ridge when my horse spooked at a snake. He threw me, and I slid off the ridge."

"You must've landed hard. You sure you didn't break anything?"

She lifted her right hand, winced as she flexed the fingers. "I think it's just sprained."

"Let me see."

Gently, Cuno took the girl's hand in his. It was soft and smooth and long-fingered, with a small cameo ring on the ring finger, a tiny amethyst inset in gold on the pinky. He squeezed the slightly swollen wrist gently with his right hand, bent it with his left.

The girl winced and sucked a shallow breath.

"I think you're right—it's just a sprain." He smiled at her. "What do you say we get you out of here?"

"That's the best idea I've heard all day."

Cuno grabbed his lariat, looped it, and dropped it first over her and then over him. Drawing her close and turning her away from him, he drew the loop tight about their waists. He only vaguely acknowledged the thrill of having the lovely girl this close to him, their hips locked together.

"Ready?"

She nodded.

"Let my horse do the work," he said, then yelled up to Renegade, "Pull, boy . . . easy . . . !"

The horse stepped forward. The rope tightened suddenly, jerking Cuno and the girl up and forward. The girl gasped as her lungs compressed.

Grabbing the rope in both hands, Cuno slammed his feet against the clay bank, yelling, "Keep going, Renny. Slow, nice and slow."

The rope tightened, drawing Cuno and the girl slowly up the slope, Cuno climbing with his feet over the rocks and around shrubs, gritting his teeth against the rope cutting into his lower back. The girl ground back against him, her thick hair wisping about his face, catching in his lips.

Renegade paused, and the girl slammed back against Cuno with a gasp, her hair clouding his eyes. The horse continued, taking up the rope's slack, jerking Cuno against her.

Her body, gently curving under the skirt and torn blouse, was soft and supple in his embrace. As uncomfortable as the situation was, with the rope seeming about to cut him in two, the feel and heat of her body made his loins tingle.

"Keep going, boy—just a little more," he yelled up the slope, hoping Renegade could hear down the other side.

As they were pulled to the butte's crest, Cuno yelled, "Easy, boy, easy . . . *stop!*"

The horse stopped, and the girl stumbled. Cuno tripped, and they fell together on the ridge top. Cuno looked up. The girl's lovely, dust-smudged face was six inches from his own, her round eyes the rich brown of mahogany.

She flushed. Cuno reached down and loosened the knot holding them together.

"You okay?" he said, throwing off the loop.

"Yes," she said, her chest heaving. "Thank you. I'm not sure what I would have done if you hadn't come along."

"It was a ticklish situation," Cuno admitted, climbing to his feet.

He offered her his hand. She took it, and he helped her to her feet. When they'd dusted themselves off, she tossed her hair back from her temples, untangling it with her fingers.

"Well, I guess we best get back to the ranch," she said.

Coiling his rope, Cuno gazed at her curiously.

"You are one of my father's riders aren't you?"

Cuno hesitated, feeling a ripple of excitement through his entire being. "Who's your father?"

"Why, Franklin Evans, of course," the girl said. "I'm Delinda, his daughter."

21

CUNO FROZE, HIS heart skipping a beat. He felt his face flush to his hair roots and hoped his tan covered it.

Evans's daughter. Who else would she be—out here in the middle of nowhere, on Evans's range?

Cuno couldn't help staring at her, wondering how such a beautiful, genteel young woman could possibly be related to Franklin and Vince Evans. What a shame.

He tried to speak. It wouldn't come. He tried again. "I'm . . . I'm not on your father's roll. I was just passin' through." His mind raced; he was thinking fast, trying to come up with an excuse for being on the Muleshoe. At the same time, he found himself planning ahead.

He might be able to use this girl to gain access to her father. The idea gave him a twinge of guilt, but only a twinge. He would not pull any punches in his war with Franklin Evans.

He added quickly, hoping it didn't look like the idea had just occurred to him, "I thought I'd stop at the ranch headquarters and see if your father was hiring riders."

Delinda Evans studied him, and he tensed. What if

she recognized him from the description on the wanted dodgers?

"I didn't think you looked familiar," she said, adding with a smile, "You look too nice."

"How's that?"

"Father hires mostly ruffians. He says he needs them to keep squatters and rustlers out, but I think it's just a habit. By now, everyone knows not to squat on Muleshoe range, or to rustle its cows." She still appraised him with a funny little half smile. "What's your name?"

Cuno blinked, maintaining a bland expression. "Kyle Morgan."

"Well, Kyle Morgan, can you shoot?"

"Can I shoot?"

"It's the first thing Father will ask. Not how well can you ride or cut calves from bulberry snags, but how well can you shoot?"

Cuno shrugged a shoulder. "I can shoot well enough."

She considered him thoughtfully. "You look tough enough, but maybe not rough enough. But your saving my life might sway you in Father's favor."

"I wouldn't exactly say I saved your life," Cuno said as he coiled his lariat, his hands shaking slightly with the prospect of finally meeting Evans face-to-face.

"I'd say you did," Delinda Evans said. "The Muleshoe is over twenty thousand acres. Do you know how long it would take Father's men to find me?"

Delinda gazed down the ridge again, and shook her head darkly. "I have a feeling I'd have been painter food on that ledge tonight . . . if you hadn't come along, Mr. Morgan."

She gave a shudder. Then, her demeanor brightened, and she smiled, brown eyes flashing. Cuno found himself liking this girl very much. She had a frank but breezy manner. She'd obviously grown up out here. He doubted she'd always been here—she owned refinement she'd no doubt gleaned from a city—but her demeanor was definitely Western.

"May I have some water?" she asked.

He'd been so caught up in the fact she was Evans's daughter, he'd forgotten to offer his canteen. "You bet, sorry."

He turned and jogged down the opposite slope, returning a minute later with Renegade in tow. He uncorked his canteen and handed it to her.

"Thank you," she said, and sipped. Several water drops dribbled over her lips, down her chin, and runneled through the light coating of dust along her neck, disappearing into her cleavage, lightly dampening her soiled blouse.

"Water never tasted so good," she said, corking the canteen and returning it to him. She wiped her mouth with the back of her hand. "I suppose my father will be getting worried. . . ."

Cuno looped the canteen over his saddle horn. "I'm ready to ride if you are."

A few minutes later, riding double on Renegade, they climbed down off the ridge, heading southeast toward the Muleshoe headquarters. Delinda asked him where he was from. He said Kansas. He told her several more lies in answer to further probing questions about his past.

"Your father hires rough men," he said as Renegade jogged over a knoll, digging his back hooves into the powdered trail. "Does that mean he's a rough man himself?"

He was doing some probing of his own, for anything he could learn about his opponent.

He felt her shrug behind him. "He settled this country himself, driving a small herd up from Texas just after the war. Only grasshoppers and Indians were here at the time, as he likes to tell it. He fought off the Indians and built his herd and made a lot of money. Not a lot of friends, but a lot of money. He has around fifteen men on his roll, and a housekeeper."

"Must be nice."

"Not all that nice. My mother left him and went back East. My brother, a chip off the old block, was killed last year by a gunslick from Nebraska."

Cuno resisted the urge to snort. "A gunslick, eh?"

"Yes, it was a cold-blooded killing, or so Father says. He says the gunman shot Vince in the back while he was crossing the street in Julesburg. Father issued a bounty for the man. If I know Father, he'll find him . . . sooner or later. Someone will tote his head back in a sack, and Father will begin sleeping again."

Cuno's gut burned at the lie, but he bit back his exasperation. "I'd imagine having your son shot down for no good reason would tear you up pretty bad."

"Yes, if that's what happened," Delinda said dryly. "Vince had fewer friends than Father, and was even better at provoking a fight." She paused. "After hearing all that, are you sure you want to work for Franklin Evans, Mr. Morgan?"

"I've worked for tough men before," Cuno said flippantly. But he stared hard at the trail ahead, anticipating the moment this lovely girl's father would enter his gunsights.

After a while, the trail curved between hills, traversed a narrow stream, and mounted an upward-slanting table peppered with grazing cattle. The ranch headquarters sprawled a thousand yards ahead, along the lower slopes of a low, sun-seared jog of dun hills with nary a tree in sight.

"So what keeps you here?" Cuno asked the girl.

He felt her shrug behind him. "I'm only visiting. I left with Mother three years ago. I'm currently attending a teaching college in Joliet, Illinois, but I return to the ranch for a few months each year. He is my father, after all. He adores me. I can't turn my back on him."

"Blood's thicker than water."

"It is at that, Mr. Morgan."

"Kyle."

"You know what, Kyle?" she asked, leaning forward to regard him wistfully over his shoulder. "I hope he hires you. I think you're nice, and we could sure use a nice man around here."

"Thank you, ma'am," he said, not liking himself a whole lot at the moment.

"Please call me Delinda."

Cuno watched as the ranch buildings spread out before him, his stomach muscles tightening and his heart quickening.

He feared he was playing into Evans's hands, but he knew of no other way to kill the son of a bitch. And that's what he'd do, even if Evans's gunslicks made him pay with his own life.

The Muleshoe compound was like most he'd seen across the West, with a half-dozen corrals flanked by haystacks, several stables surrounded with work wagons in various stages of repair, a blacksmith shop puffing sooty black smoke from its tin chimney pipe, and a long, low bunkhouse of square-hewn logs and cedar shakes.

Horses milled in the corrals, and chickens pecked in the yard. The air smelled of coal smoke and manure.

Sitting back from the main compound, separated from the other buildings by a good sixty yards, the house was everything Cuno had expected, and more. It was vast and low, built of stone. Tall, arched windows, wrought-iron grillwork, and the spacious flagstone terraces surrounding the house added a Spanish flavor. The red tile roofing shimmered in the sun dropping behind a dark jog of western hills and mesas.

As Cuno and the girl rode toward the wrought-iron hitch rack, a dog's deep, inquiring bark rolled up from their right. Turning, Cuno saw several men gathered before a stable. Most of the cowboys were mounted on quarter horses outfitted with rifles snugged in saddle boots. Two men were still afoot. All were looking toward Cuno and Delinda.

The dog stood near the group, staring at the newcomers with its ears laid back and tail erect. The tall, black Rottweiler barked again, sounding like howitzer fire and making several horses jerk.

"Delinda!" one of the men yelled scoldingly, and began walking toward them.

Limped would be a more accurate description. Apparently, the man's left leg would bend only slightly at the knee, so he had to kick it out and swing it around as he stepped forward with his right.

He was a burly little terrier in late middle age, wearing baggy trousers, white shirt, and a green duck coat. A long, thin cigar was clamped in one side of his mouth. He had a considerable paunch, and his shoulders sagged, but Cuno sensed he'd been a powerful man at one time. Probably still was. Cuno remembered the grisly scars on Minnie's back.

The dog walked beside Evans, fiery eyes pinned on Cuno, panting.

The man who'd been standing with Evans walked this way, as well, quickly catching up with the short man with no effort at all. This man was tall, slab-chested, and dressed in traditional cowboy garb, with an oiled Colt hanging low on his thigh. His flat-brimmed hat was a tattered, weather-stained Stetson with a concho band. He had black hair and small, shadowy eyes set wide and deep along a broad, scarred nose. A hard case doubling as Evans's segundo, no doubt.

"I'm all right, Dad," the girl called as Cuno gave her a hand down from Renegade's rear.

"Where in the blue hell have you been!" Franklin Evans barked as he hurried toward her, awkwardly swinging his leg, breathing hard with the effort. "Gypsum came home riderless fifteen minutes ago, and I've been worried sick! Me and the boys were about to go lookin'!"

The limp took Cuno by surprise. He hadn't heard about that. Somehow, he'd pictured Evans as a big, stern man dressed all in black, with a silver-plated revolver on his hip and wearing a wide, high-crowned Stetson. Maybe Cuno had just wanted him to be that way, so it would be more satisfying to take the man down. He felt a twinge of disappointment. But the man's diminutive size and limp did not change the fact that he was a venal liar and a cold-blooded killer.

It did not change the fact that he would die.

"I'm sorry I worried you, Dad," Delinda said. "I was riding along Alder Gulch when Gypsum spooked at a snake, and threw me. I tumbled down a butte and got stranded on a ledge."

"Stranded?" the old, crippled bulldog barked with exasperation. "Are you hurt?"

Delinda shook her head. "Just sprained my wrist, got a few scrapes and bruises. I'll be fine." She turned to indicate Cuno still sitting atop Renegade. "Fortunately, this young man came along and rescued me."

As though Evans hadn't heard her—he had yet to acknowledge Cuno's presence with so much as a glance—he said, "Delinda, you have to stop riding off by yourself. If I told you once, I told you a thousand times, this is no country in which young women can ride off alone and not expect trouble from snakes or falling rock or cutthroats or Injuns! I know you get bored when you're home, but by Ned, you'll just have to limit your prowling to the compound. Is that clear?"

The girl did not shrink from the impassioned onslaught. She paled slightly, but said simply, "Let's talk about that later, shall we? In the meantime, I'd like you to meet the man who saved your daughter's delicate hide." She turned to Cuno with a warm, ironic smile. "Kyle Morgan, meet my father, Franklin Evans."

Gravely self-conscious, wondering if Evans would recognize him from the descriptions he'd no doubt heard in Julesburg, Cuno regarded his nemesis icily behind an innocuous smile.

"Pleasure."

"Thank you, Mr. Morgan, for helping my daughter," Evans said in his raspy, strangely high-pitched voice. "I sincerely appreciate that."

"I was happy to do it, Mr. Evans."

"This is Brand Tuttle," Delinda said, a shadow crossing her features as she nodded to indicate the tall, dark-haired gent beside Evans. "He's father's ramrod."

"Good to meet you," Cuno said.

Tuttle said nothing, just stood towering over his boss, regarding Cuno flintily. The dog sat between them, panting and eyeing Cuno like a fresh bone.

Evans's voice tightened. "Mr. Morgan, I am indeed obliged to you for helping my daughter out of a pinch, but I'll also have to ask what you were doing on Muleshoe range. My land is strictly forbidden to outsiders."

"Dad!" Delinda objected, her face coloring with genuine anger. "I don't—"

"Hush!" Evans scolded, this time effectively cowing the girl.

He turned his interrogative gaze back to Cuno, who shrugged and cracked another smile.

His right hand was on his knee, but he was ready to slap his gun if the need arose, and start firing until the Colt was empty, giving the first two shots to old Evans himself, crippled or not.

"Lookin' for a job, Mr. Evans," he said innocently. "I thought maybe you'd be hiring for the fall gather."

"Dad," Delinda said, jumping in before her father could respond, "I've invited Kyle to stay at the Muleshoe tonight, as a way of repaying him for his assistance. Please give him a chance."

Fidgety, Evans looked at his hard-faced ramrod, then at Delinda. She leveled a beseeching, vaguely chiding gaze at him. Evans furled his brows and chewed his lip. "I won't promise anything, young man, but I guess I owe you a listen."

With that, the old man turned and started dragging his leg to the house. "Come on, Devil," he called without turning around. The dog tore its hungry gaze from Cuno and followed Evans to the front portal, leaving Cuno, Delinda, and Brand Tuttle milling in awkward silence.

Delinda smiled at Cuno. Brand Tuttle stared up at Cuno coldly. Finally, Tuttle turned to Delinda, cracking a smile that would have looked as natural on a granite mountain wall.

"Sure am glad you weren't hurt bad, Miss Delinda,"

Tuttle muttered. He kept his stony gaze on the girl for a full five seconds, his lips stretched unnaturally, grinding strange lines around his eyes.

Delinda appeared to recoil inwardly, clasping her hands before her. "Thank you, Brand," she said, unable to meet his eyes.

Tuttle pinched his hat brim to her, and lifted his gaze to Cuno once more. "You can stable your own horse," he growled. "B stable yonder," he said, jerking a thumb to indicate a low building on the other side of the blacksmith shed.

Then he turned and walked back toward the A stable, before which the ranch hands were unsaddling their horses.

Cuno looked at Delinda, who watched the ramrod amble stiffly across the hard-packed compound. She clasped her shoulders as though chilled, and shuddered.

22

DELINDA EVANS WATCHED Brand Tuttle
disappear into the stable. When she had regained her wits,
she turned to Cuno, astraddle Renegade and watching her
curiously.

"When you've stabled your horse," she said, "come back
to the house. Father will probably nap until supper time, but
I can offer you a cup of fresh, hot coffee in the kitchen."

"Fresh, hot coffee sounds fine."

She smiled, gave another cool glance at Tuttle's retreating back, then turned for the house. Cuno watched her go,
thinking how she belonged here about as much as he did.
Finally, he turned Renegade into the yard and gave him a
good long water at the main stock tank, from which clear,
cold water ran from a pipe as the tin blades rattled overhead.

When the horse had had his fill, Cuno used his neckerchief to wash his face, chest, and the back of his neck, running wet fingers through his hair. Finally, he led Cuno over
to the B stable, opened the double doors, and stepped inside, where the air was heavy with the smell of fresh-cut
timothy, oats, and ammonia. Several horses stood back in

the shadowed stalls, but most were empty. The stable was no doubt used for the riders' second-string mounts and those that needed doctoring.

"Didn't want you in with their A string, Renegade," Cuno told the horse as he led him down the runway. "Imagine that. . . ."

When he'd led Renegade into a stall about halfway down, he unsaddled him, setting all his tack on the stall partition, then forked fresh hay into the stall and used some to give the horse a good rubdown. Renegade's muscles rippled at Cuno's hard scrubbing, and he nickered occasionally and stomped his back hooves with pleasure.

While he rubbed the horse, Cuno thought through his options here at the Muleshoe. It was a tricky situation, made more complicated by the presence of Evans's daughter. He wouldn't kill the man in front of her. He'd wait until he and the old man were alone sometime this evening, maybe when Evans was grilling him about the job.

Better yet, he'd find a way to gag Evans and lead him off the ranch under cover of darkness. A safe distance from the headquarters, he could take his time, explain to him about his son's attempt to murder an innocent pleasure girl . . . explain to him about July . . . hear Evans beg for his life . . . make the killing last a good, long time. . . .

A shadow moved to Cuno's right, and he turned to look. A man stood in the open doorway, silhouetted against the dusky light. A big, broad-shouldered man wearing a flat-brimmed hat. One of the conchos around the crown caught a vagrant shaft of salmon light and flashed.

"Hello, pilgrim." The voice owned the deep, taut, rhythmless rhythm of Brand Tuttle.

"Hidy-ho," Cuno said with false cheer. He stood watching Tuttle over the top of the horse stalls, peering around the one horse in his way.

"Came to teach you how it is here on the Muleshoe."

Cuno let a few seconds slip. "Thoughtful of you."

Tuttle started down the runway with his swaggering gait, arms hanging straight at his sides like his hands were weighted down with iron. Cuno dropped the hay he'd been using on Renegade and stepped into the runway.

As he spread his feet strategically, the doors behind scraped, the hinges squeaking. Cuno glanced over his shoulder as another silhouetted figure stepped into the stall, paused as he looked around, eyes adjusting, then made his way toward Cuno. He was even taller and broader than Tuttle.

Cuno smiled. "It takes two to teach this lesson, I reckon."

"Sometimes, if I wanna teach it real good," Tuttle said.

The two men wasted no time. Cuno looked first one way, then the other. He hesitated, knowing it would be a mistake to pull his gun. . . . Before he knew it, Tuttle had said, "Grab him, Ham," and broad, strong hands pinned his arms behind his back. Cuno struggled to free himself, grunting and cursing, to no avail.

Tuttle moved up to him, brought his right arm back, then forward with all the power of a steam locomotive's piston, burying his fist deep in Cuno's solar plexus. The air gushed out of Cuno's lungs, and he dropped forward at the waist, sagging at the knees. He would have fallen, but the big man behind held him up.

Ham was strong. Damn strong. He smelled like sweat and leather and hot iron and coal smoke. The ranch's blacksmith, no doubt—brought in when some hard muscle was needed in one of Tuttle's "lessons."

Cuno sucked air, or tried to. He felt like a fish flopping around on shore. The pain was excruciating. He felt like he'd been run over by a lumber dray.

"That was just to get your attention," Tuttle said. "Ready to listen?"

Cuno's only reply was to gasp and suck at the same time. His lungs felt shriveled as raisins. His head swam for lack of oxygen.

"Good," Tuttle rumbled. "Lesson *numero uno*: No one messes with Delinda Evans. Got it? No one. She's mine.

Tonight, I so much as see you smile at her across the table, you're a dead man."

Tuttle glanced at the man behind Cuno. "Ham, knock lesson number one home for me, will you?"

Ham released Cuno's right hand long enough to jab him hard in the right kidney. Cuno was going down to the floor when Ham caught him with both hands and yanked him up. His entire side burned, but at least he was sucking air.

"Lesson *numero dos*," Tuttle said. "Mr. Evans is prob'ly gonna give you a job, 'cause he can't say no to Miss Delinda. You're gonna have a change of heart. Understand? Tomorrow, you're gonna decide you got the sudden itch to head to Wyoming, and you're gonna ride out of here like a jackass with cans tied to its tail." Tuttle paused for emphasis. "Understand?"

Cuno grunted and groaned as the pain in his gut and the pain in his back connected to make one hell of a flare.

"I asked if you understood."

Cuno knew he was about to take another lick. He also knew the smartest thing would be to take it and live to fight another day . . . but that wasn't how he was made.

Summoning strength from some reserve, he did the only thing possible at the moment, lifting his right foot and connecting it soundly with Brand Tuttle's oysters.

Tuttle bent forward with a grunt, his face coloring up like a Dakota sunset, grabbing his crotch. Meanwhile, Cuno tried again to wrestle out of Ham's grip, but he would have had an easier time trying to free himself from a corn picker.

When Tuttle lifted his face, his eyes were wide and glistening, his teeth bared. "Hold him steady, Ham." Tuttle straightened, drew his fist back, and slammed it forward, connecting squarely with Cuno's left cheek. His face now sending up a flair of pain to add to the others, he flew back against the blacksmith's leather-covered chest.

"Easy, easy," Ham said. "Don't wanna mess up his face before supper." The big man's shoulders heaved with a chuckle. "Might upset the girl."

"Shut up," Tuttle said.

Ham fell silent.

Tuttle looked at Cuno. "You had enough, pretty boy? Or should I mess up your face so bad, Delinda won't recognize you from Adam's off-ox?"

Cuno winced at the pain in his cheekbone, tipped his head forward as he hung in the blacksmith's arms. He shook his head. "I've had enough." There was no point in taking a beating when he didn't need to.

Tuttle removed the Colt Frontier from Cuno's holster and wedged it behind his own cartridge belt, saying, "The old man don't allow firearms in the house. You can pick this up from me when you leave bright and early tomorrow."

When he'd removed Cuno's holster from his rifle boot, resting the rifle barrel on his shoulder, Tuttle said to Ham, "Let him go."

Ham's hands opened. Cuno staggered sideways and grabbed a stanchion, crouching there over his tender belly, massaging the equally tender kidney while blinking against the swelling around his eye.

"See you at dinner," Tuttle said. He and Ham swaggered out the front. Ham was chuckling.

Cuno winced and straightened, stretching his back. What bothered him more than his aches and pains was his missing weapons. Without them, he was helpless.

Moving into Renegade's stall, he rummaged through his saddlebags until he came up with a spare Smith & Wesson five-shooter. After checking it for ammo, he lifted his right pants leg, dropped the pocket pistol into his boot, and lowered his denims over the slight bulge.

When Cuno had stowed his empty holster and cartridge belt in his saddlebags, he headed for the Evans house, the windows dimly lit against the gathering night. If he'd felt like a Christian led to the lions before, he thought he was now beginning to hear the lions roar. Only he wasn't being led—by anything more than his hunger for vengeance, that is.

He was doing this to himself, and he was beginning to doubt he was doing much more than getting himself killed.

He knocked on the heavy-timbered front door. Not receiving an answer, he went in. After several minutes of wandering around the high-ceilinged rooms filled with heavy wood furniture, expensive lamps, and occasional game trophies looming from the paneled walls, he found the dining room. A long, dark-oak table stretched between a newly laid fire in a giant hearth and a row of tall, arched windows, the heavy shutters thrown back to the mild night. The table was set for dining.

Pots and pans clattered behind a swing door. Succulent, spicy aromas drifted through the cracks around the door. Cuno tapped on it lightly.

"Uh, Miss Delinda?"

Her soft voice sounded through the door. "Come."

He pushed through the door and stood looking around the kitchen, more vast than most sitting parlors he'd seen. It was equipped with two ranges large as Murphy wagons, and several cabinets and worktables. Delinda sat at the largest table, balling dough into cookies. A gray-haired Chinese man clad in a deer-hide, wool-lined vest over a puffy white shirt tended a smoking cast-iron skillet at the range on the opposite end of the room. Delinda, seeing Cuno's face, stopped rolling dough and gazed up at him with alarm.

"Oh, my God, what happened?" she exclaimed, dropping the dough as she stood and came toward him, her gaze riveted to the swelling around his eye.

"Went back to school for a bit. Is that coffee offer still good?"

Delinda stopped a few feet away from him, her features turning angry. "Brand."

"He's set his hat for you . . . in case you haven't noticed."

Delinda's jaws tightened and her eyes slitted, her face bleaching with rage. Balling her fists, she moved stiffly to a range where a percolator bubbled, grabbed a china cup off a shelf just above her head, and filled it. Her hair was still damp from a bath. It fell in ringlets to her shoulders. She wore a blue, wasp-wasted dress cut low enough to show the round curves of alabaster breasts.

Turning to Cuno, she said, "Sit down," indicating the table at which she'd been making cookies.

Cuno sat down gingerly, wincing against the pain wracking eighty percent of his body. He'd fought many men for sport back in Nebraska, but none who'd packed a punch like Brand Tuttle's.

Delinda set the cup before him, then wheeled away, saying, "I'll get some cold water for that eye."

Cuno grabbed her wrist, stopping her. "Forget it," he said gently. "It's gonna swell no matter what."

"That man!" she exclaimed, coloring.

The Chinese cook turned toward her, a grim smile on his long, pale face. "That Brand, he no good for you, Miss Delinda. No good!"

Delinda said, still regarding his bruised eye with distress, "Kyle, meet Hung Chow, father's cook and housekeeper."

Cuno nodded.

"That Brand Tuttle," Hung Chow said, wielding a spatula furiously from across the room, "he no good for Miss Delinda. He no good for anyone. No, no, no!"

"I know," Delinda said, pinching more dough from the main ball and resuming her work.

"I take it you're turning away his attentions," Cuno asked, blowing ripples on the hot, black coffee.

"It's not that simple," Delinda said, peeling the potato with slightly more vigor than necessary. "Dad would like me to marry Brand and settle here, forget about teaching altogether. He'd like for me and Brand to take over the ranch, so he can relax and play cards all day in Julesburg. I guess you noticed his leg."

"Accident?"

Delinda nodded. "Three years ago, a hay wagon slammed into him while the men were putting hay up in the barn. The driver hadn't set the brake, and the mules spooked. Shattered the knee. Now arthritis is setting in, adding to the misery. I think it's partly what's making him so mean."

"What was Vince's excuse?" Cuno wanted to ask, but resisted, sipping the coffee instead.

"Well, you better keep your feet greased," Cuno said. "It don't look like Brand's gonna give up anytime soon."

"No, and neither is my father," Delinda said, setting another wad of dough on the cookie sheet.

A cloud suddenly passed over her beautiful, oval face. She reached across the table, placed both her hands on his arm, and gazed up at him with gravity. "I'm sorry for bringing you here. I was lonely and brought you here for my own selfish reasons. I should have discouraged you and sent you on your way. You don't want to work for my father, Kyle." Her expression hardened. "You don't want to work for Brand Tuttle."

Cuno wasn't sure how to answer that. Emotions fought within him, and guilt seemed to be winning. She was a decent, innocent girl, and he was using her hospitality to kill her father.

He placed his hand on hers and gazed back at her, deciding a subject change was due. "How's the wrist?"

As she gazed at him, her eyes turned from tender to vaguely puzzled. Finally, she took her hands away, leaning slowly back in her chair. "Better."

The loud chimes of a grandfather clock sounded from the dining room. The Chinese cook muttered with alarm.

"It's six," Delinda said to Cuno. "Father will be at the table shortly. Would you mind distracting him for a few minutes? It's been a busy day here. . . . Father sent word that we have another guest. Hung had to prepare another chicken."

"You bet," Cuno said, rising.

"Oh, and Kyle," Delinda said as he headed for the swing door.

Cuno turned around.

"Brand dines with us."

"Thanks for the warning." He turned and pushed through the door and froze.

At the heavy-timbered table sat the wizened Evans and Brand Tuttle. To Tuttle's right sat the unexpected guest—a man so large that he made even Tuttle look small. A man with an enormous, scarred face covered with a beard that was brown on one cheek, alkali-white on the other.

From beneath the white beard, a birthmark swirled up into his forehead, ending in an odd, pink curl. The man's thick salt-and-pepper hair lay tangled and matted about his head, showing the creases left by a hat.

What the hell was Ruben Pacheca doing here?

Cuno's heart drummed.

23

THE ROTTWEILER SITTING beside Evans growled, nostrils expanding and contracting as it tested the air, snake eyes glistening. Sitting at the head of the table, in a tall-backed chair, Evans turned to Cuno and lowered a calming hand to the dog's head.

"Easy, Devil, easy," Evans said. "Mr. Morgan, there you are. Won't you join us?" He turned away and turned back sharply. "Good Lord!" he exclaimed. "What happened to your eye?"

Cuno looked at Tuttle, who sat with his hands clasped on the table, a villainous grin pulling at his mouth. His eyes flashed a warning.

"Just had a little run-in with a . . . swing door," Cuno said.

Evans followed Cuno's gaze to Tuttle. Evans's own smile grew as the light of realization flickered in his eyes. "I see, I see. You've met Brand." He chuckled and shifted his gaze to the giant sitting to Brand Tuttle's right. "Morgan, meet Ruben Pacheca. The best bounty hunter on the frontier. When I heard he was in town, I invited him out here for supper."

"Oh?" Cuno said, his innocent smile in place as he

pulled out a chair and sat down across from Pacheca. "You favor bounty hunters, do you, Mr. Evans?" Pacheca's presence had started a high-pitched ringing in his ears. He had no idea how he was going to play this joker in a new game with all different rules.

"Only the best ones," Evans said. "And only since my son was gunned down in cold blood in Julesburg."

Cuno nodded. "Miss Delinda told me about that." He leaned forward, stretching his right hand across the table at Pacheca, ingratiating himself. "Pleased to meet you. Heard a lot about you."

The giant gave Cuno's hand a jerk, grunting, and sat back in his chair. His eyes met Cuno's for only a moment, then scuttled away. He was the size of a bear, but his demeanor was more like that of a coyote's. Wily and shy. He looked about as comfortable in Evans's lodge as would any wild animal. But Cuno didn't think anyone had recognized him.

Not yet, anyway.

Evans turned to the bounty hunter and resumed their conversation. "Now then, Pacheca, you mentioned you'd been hunting Cuno Massey—for which I'm eternally grateful, I might add. If that is indeed the case, what brought you to Julesburg, if I may ask?"

The giant sat stiffly back in his chair, blinking his eyes slowly. "Him," he said with a grunt, as though he'd been asked an utterly stupid question.

"Him?" Evans glanced at Tuttle, befuddled, then looked back at Pacheca. His expression was incredulous. "You think Cuno Massey is in Julesburg?"

"He's somewhere around here," Pacheca said in his slow, guttural drawl. "I trailed him outta Canyon City over Colorada-way. Got waylaid by a couple bastards who stole my horse when I was havin' trouble with a tooth. When I finally got my mount back, his trail was cold."

The giant wrinkled his nostrils pridefully. "I cut it again, anyway. Wasn't that hard. Sure as shit up a cow's ass, it led right to Julesburg."

Tuttle glanced at his boss, skeptical. "What in the hell would he be doin' in Julesburg?"

Pacheca chuffed. "It don't take a fuckin' pencil pusher to figure it out. He's here lookin' fer you." The bounty hunter smiled with his eyes at Evans, as though the whole thing delighted him no end.

Evans scowled, his craggy cheeks flushing. "For me?"

"I don't think he's here lookin' for the Virgin Mary."

Evans glanced around at the windows. "Brand, close the shutters."

Tuttle slid his chair back, stood, drew the shutters closed, and locked them. Evans sat tensely, his square, gray head reaching only halfway up the tall chair back, his eyes darting nervously over the covered windows. The room had grown darker and the candles and lamps flickered.

Feeling even more trapped, Cuno wished like hell he had his Colt.

To Tuttle, Evans said, barking out the orders with an air of grave thoughtfulness, "Send five men to town. Right now. Tonight. Tell them not to come back until they've found Massey. Post another five men about the grounds at all times between now until Massey's caught."

"You got it, Boss." Tuttle marched out of the room.

"He must be mad!" Evans exclaimed with exasperation, leaning forward in his chair, planting his elbows on the table, and running his hands across his face. "Pure mad."

Pacheca grunted a laugh, massive shoulders bobbing. Like Cuno, he was enjoying the wealthy rancher's unease.

"What's he gonna do?" Evans asked no one in particular. "Ride in here, guns blazing?"

Evans turned to the bounty hunter. "Mr. Pacheca, let me make the bounty on that killer's head a little more lucrative. If you can bring me his head in twenty-four hours—just twenty-four hours!—I'll double it."

Pacheca's lips bunched, the knobs of his scarred cheeks rose, slitting his stony eyes. "That a promise?"

"You want it in writing?"

"No, I want it."

Evans scowled at him, puzzled. "Huh?"

"I want it right here, right now." Pacheca slid his eyes to the bone china before him. "You can set it right here on this fancy plate."

Evans had no idea what the man was talking about, and his expression said so.

Cuno knew, however.

Reading Pacheca's eyes, which did not slide to him, he suddenly bolted up in his chair, threw himself to his left, and rolled.

Out of the corner of his vision, he saw Pacheca bolt to his feet, his chair blowing back against the wall behind him, and lift a sawed-off rifle to his waist. At the same time, Evans's dog flew at Cuno—a black, snarling blur.

Pacheca's rifle cracked twice. One slug tore up the carpet a foot off Cuno's right hip. The second slammed into the dog, who gave a sharp yelp and rolled in a dead heap against a sideboard.

Rolling off a shoulder and jerking the five-shot Smith & Wesson from his boot, Cuno came to his feet, crouching and turning toward Pacheca.

The bounty hunter shouted, "Die, you son of a bitch!" as he triggered two more shots, the slugs curling the air around Cuno's head before they slammed into the cabinets behind him, breaking lamps and vases. The reports hadn't died when Cuno extended the pocket gun and fired as Pacheca was levering another shell in his Winchester's breech.

Pop, pop! barked the Smith & Wesson.

The two bullets thumped into the big bounty hunter's chest. Pacheca tensed and staggered back two steps. Shock and surprise widening his eyes and mouth, he glanced down at his homespun tunic. He dropped the Winchester and clawed at the holes as though they were bramble burrs he could wipe away.

He staggered back against the curtained windows, shouting, *"Uhhh—God!"* and dropped to his knees. He was falling forward when Cuno slid his gaze to Evans.

The rancher had stood leaning against the table, staring in shock as Cuno and the bounty hunter had swapped lead. As he met Cuno's gaze, realization suddenly dawned on him. Wild-eyed, he grabbed a slim, serrated knife from beside his plate. Kicking his crippled leg, he lunged forward, red-faced and raging, coming at Cuno like a wounded bull from the chute.

Coolly, Cuno leveled the Smithy at him.

Evans froze and stared at the gun.

"I'm Cuno Massey, you son of a bitch. You murdered my wife, made my life a living hell, and I've been waiting a long time for this."

With that, he pulled the trigger, blowing a neat round hole through Evans's throat. It stopped the old man in his tracks. The rancher dropped the knife and grabbed his throat with both hands, eyes wide with shock and terror.

Cuno fired again, blowing a hole through the rancher's forehead, throwing the man backward off his feet. Dead in midair, Evans hit the floor hard with a deafening boom, making the room quake.

Spying movement to his right, he turned. Delinda stood before the swinging doors, shuttling a wide-eyed, disbelieving gaze across the smoky room. It caught on her father, lingered there, then turned to Cuno. Hung Chow poked his head through the swinging door behind her, a wary cast to his thin, gray features.

"I killed your brother because he was about to slit a pleasure girl's throat," Cuno told Delinda, holding the warm pocket pistol down at his side. "Your father's bounty hunters killed my wife."

Delinda stared at him. She swallowed and turned to her father, walking slowly toward him. Tears filled her eyes and slowly spilled over as she stood staring down at him. Behind her, Hung Chow muttered unintelligibly under his breath.

Excited voices rose outside.

Delinda turned to Cuno. "Go," she said firmly. "Leave before they kill you." Looking at her father again, she said dully, "There's been enough killing."

He'd seen an outside door in the kitchen, and he moved to it now, stopping at the swing door and glancing back at Delinda Evans staring down at her dead father.

"Just go," she said coldly, not turning to him.

He doubted he'd make it. He had only one bullet left in the S&W, but he had to try. He wanted to live, he realized as he ran into the kitchen, nearly running into the Chinese cook, and opened the outside door.

Stepping slowly out, he looked carefully from side to side.

"Wait." He whipped around. Delinda stood in the kitchen. Quickly, she threw an Oriental rug back, revealing a trapdoor with a metal ring. Kneeling, she grabbed the ring and lifted the door. "Hide in the cellar. Hurry. I'll distract them."

Cuno stared at her. The cook stood on the far side of the room, muttering and wringing his gnarled hands. Evans's riders were in the house now, yelling, their boots pounding. Brand Tuttle's voice boomed above the others.

Cuno bolted to the rectangular hole, dropped down the short, steep stairs. Crouching on the cellar floor, where the cool air smelled of dirt and potatoes, he looked up at the lighted opening. Delinda eased the door down, sealing the hole in darkness.

Boots pounded over head. He blinked his eyes against the fine dust sifting from the rafters.

"He ran out the back!" Delinda yelled, her voice edged with exasperation. "He's probably heading for the creek. *Get after him!*"

Several of the men cursed and ran, the commotion nearly deafening in the cellar. When they were all outside, Brand Tuttle's muffled voice lifted. "He's headin' toward the creek! Spread out—we'll cut him off!"

When nearly a minute had passed, the door opened. Cuno blinked his eyes against the sudden light, and climbed the five steps to the kitchen. Delinda stood regarding him soberly. "Saddle your horse and get out. Get off the Muleshoe, and please don't ever come back."

Cuno gazed at her, his heart breaking for her. "Delinda, I'm—"

"Oh, just go!" she cried, turning her back and covering her face with her hands, sobs wracking her.

Knowing there was nothing more he could say, he turned and left the kitchen, hurrying through the dining room toward the front door. A carved door stood half open at the end of the wide hall, and he made for it. The room had a big oak desk and several leather chairs. A gun rack sporting hunting rifles and shotguns hung to the left of a stucco fireplace.

Most of the weapons, including a Maynard Creedmoor, were too fancy for Cuno's purposes. He removed the lowest rifle—a tack-decorated .44/40 Winchester repeater—then rummaged in a cabinet for shells. He found a box with twenty or so shells. They'd have to do. He didn't have time to search for more.

Quickly loading the rifle, he dropped the excess shells in his pocket and made for the front door. Outside, he looked around. The bunkhouse windows were lit, but the yard was empty and silent. All the men had headed for the creek.

Figuring he had ten minutes at the most before Evans's men returned, he ran to the stable and wasted no time saddling Renegade. Stowing the Winchester in his rifle boot, he led the horse out the front doors, mounted up, and gigged him toward the entrance gate.

A man yelled, "Hey, there he is!"

Cuno jerked a look to his right. Coming around the house were the silhouettes of several men.

Cuno put his head down and heeled Renegade hard through the entrance gate. The horse stretched out, its hooves eating up the ground in a lunging gallop, instinctively knowing they were in trouble. Behind, several pistols cracked and yells rose.

Cuno lowered his head further, the horse's mane whipping his face. "Come on, boy! Run like hell!"

The horse responded, gobbling up the trail toward Julesburg for a full twenty minutes. When he'd climbed a low hill, Cuno reined the paint to a badly needed halt. The horse was sweat-lathered and blowing, its withers rippling with exhaustion.

Resting the horse under the star-washed sky, Cuno pricked his ears. For several minutes he heard nothing but an owl hooting in a brushy cut on the other side of the hill. A slight breeze rustled the bluestem along the trail.

Cuno was about to dismount to give the horse some water, but froze, pricking his ears once again. In the eastern distance rose the unmistakable rattle of galloping horses.

Cuno cursed, his heart drumming. They couldn't be that close. Evans's riders hadn't had enough time to saddle their horses to be this hot on his trail. But then he remembered that Evans had ordered five riders to town, which meant five horses had probably already been saddled and ready to go when Pacheca had fired on Cuno.

Five men. The others were no doubt close behind.

But if his horse was tired, theirs would be as well. Deciding to try to outrun them, he reined Renegade back toward Julesburg, digging his spurs into the horse's flanks. Tired as he was, Renegade leapt off his back feet, lurching forward in an all-out run.

Following the trail, horse and rider traced a winding path across the night-shrouded, rolling prairie, curving around buttes, rising over hillocks, and descending into creek bottoms. The cool night air beat against him, making his eyes water. All he heard was Renegade's pounding hooves. He didn't take the time to stop and listen for Muleshoe riders.

He'd just climbed a ridge on the other side of a creek when the worst happened. Renegade lurched forward and down as his right front hoof plunged into a gopher hole.

24

SCREAMING, THE HORSE rolled, throwing Cuno clear. He hit the sage-tufted ground hard, feeling a sharp pain lance his right shoulder. He rolled twice and came to rest on his back, blinking bewilderedly up at the stars, his head swimming.

Knowing the Muleshoe riders were closing, he pushed himself to his feet. His worst injury seemed to be a bruised shoulder. The leg that had been pierced by Kiowa arrows screamed with pain.

Renegade stood to trailside, reins dangling, saddle hanging down his right shoulder. Praying the horse hadn't broken its leg, Cuno bent to probe the hock with his fingers. Already the warm flesh was swelling, but the horse did not react when he dug his fingers in. Probably just a sprain, but when he led the horse in a slow circle and saw the pronounced limp, his stomach sank.

Renegade might be led back to town at a slow walk, but he wasn't being ridden anywhere.

Cuno cursed under his breath. Beginning to hear the thuds of galloping riders behind him, he led the limping horse fifty yards off the trail, angling back toward the

ravine. When he found a game trail, he led the horse down
through shrubs to the rocky bottom.

He paused behind a cottonwood growing along the trickling stream upon which starlight flickered. While Renegade
lowered his head to drink, Cuno shucked Evans's Winchester from the saddle boot, quietly jacked a shell in the chamber, and sidled up to the cottonwood, peering north to where
the trail crossed the stream about fifty yards away.

The thuds of racing hooves grew. Shadows flickered
straight downstream, starlight glancing off spurs and gun
iron. Horses splashed across the stream, and in the quiet
night Cuno could hear the riders' rasping breaths as their
horses clattered up the opposite bank, heading toward Julesburg.

Holding the tack-studded carbine in both sweaty hands,
Cuno waited. Finally, more hoofbeats rose in the east, the
noise growing in volume until Cuno could tell this was a
larger pack than the first—ten or so riders. He picked out
Brand Tuttle's voice issuing epithets and orders as the
horses splashed across the stream. A few minutes later, the
din was muffled by distance until it faded altogether.

Cuno heaved a relieved sigh. The Muleshoe men would
probably get all the way to town before they realized they
were no longer on his trail.

It was a fleeting relief. Though he was relatively safe for
the moment, he was out here in the middle of nowhere,
short on supplies, with a gimpy horse and only about
twenty shells for an unfamiliar gun.

He slid the carbine into his saddle boot, grabbed the
paint's reins, and began leading him downstream between
the eroded clay banks. The stream and ravine traced a serpentine cut through the prairie, the canyon sporadically
opening and closing, the walls lowering to reveal stars
along the horizon, then gradually closing again, blotting
out the sky. To cover his trail, Cuno led the limping horse
through the water except where it rippled into deep pools.

He'd walked for a half hour before the canyon widened
and filled with pinnacled rock formations—towering bells

and pillars of worn sandstone amidst which coyotes and occasional wolves howled in the distance. He traced a winding course through the spires, turned down a corridor away from the stream, and found a brushy hollow.

He loosened Renegade's cinch, shucked the carbine, and left the horse free to forage on the clumps of brome and needle grasses growing amongst the rocks and along the banks. Kicking coyote scat out of the way, he sat down, rested his back against a sandstone wall, and shut his eyes, intending only to doze.

When he opened them, wan morning sunlight angled over the shaded eastern walls, and mud swallows screeched. Cuno blinked, his heart thudding. He'd heard something.

There it was again—the crunch of boots on gravel.

A shadow moved along the wall before him and to the right. A second later, a man appeared—short, round-faced, wearing a dirty gray Stetson. Another man appeared beside him. They were both holding Winchesters across their chests.

Seeing Cuno, the man in the dirty Stetson stopped suddenly, eyes widening in shock. "There he is!"

As the man lowered his Winchester, Cuno raised his own carbine and fired. The gun felt awkward in his hands. The shot took the gunman in the knee. He gave a yelp and dropped. Cuno threw himself sideways as the second man fired on him, two slugs blasting the wall and spewing sand.

Cuno levered a shell and fired, levered another and fired again. He wasn't sure which shot hit the gunman, but as he lowered the carbine, he watched the man fall on his back, yelling and groaning, twisting onto his side, blood flashing in the morning light. The knee-shot man cried out and reached for his dropped rifle. Cuno extended the carbine and shot him through the back of his neck.

Cuno's heart did somersaults as he pressed his back against the sandstone wall and pushed himself to his feet. Angry shouts rose from the direction in which the two gunmen had come, from back toward the stream. Hooves pounded.

Cuno whipped his head around, looking for an escape route. The walls of the canyon were too steep for quick scaling. By the time he'd climbed a few feet, the Muleshoe men would have turned him into wolf bait.

He was boxed in. The only thing to do was stand and fight, take as many of Evans's henchmen down as he could.

Shadows appeared on the north wall as men ran toward him, jacking shells into their rifle breeches. Soon, more would appear on the ridges overhead, boxing him in even tighter. Crouching, Cuno levered his own rifle and lifted the gun to his shoulder. He was about to die, and the knowledge was a hot knot in the pit of his gut, a metallic taste on the back of his tongue.

But he'd be damned if he wouldn't take a few Muleshoe riders along for the ride. . . .

A man in a black Stetson and blue shirt appeared around a bend in the corridor, pistol extended, a savage glare in his close-set eyes. Before he could trigger the pistol, Cuno shot him, blowing him backward and out of sight with a scream. Cuno levered another round in his chamber, watching another shadow move toward him along the wall, hearing boots crunching gravel.

They were closing in. . . .

Suddenly, gunfire rose from the direction of the stream—a cacophony of several rifles and pistols fired at once. The shadow on the wall froze, then jerked, and bolted back the way it had come.

Yelling rose again, but not so much with anger as surprise.

Confused, Cuno remained crouching, fingering the carbine's trigger, shuttling his gaze from the corridor leading up from the stream to the ridges above, watching for Muleshoe men. They didn't come. Instead, he heard the clatter and pops of pistol and rifle fire, as though a small war were being waged in the main canyon.

Men cursed and screamed, grunted as though hit by flying lead.

Finally, Cuno straightened and walked toward the stream, keeping his rifle up close to his chest, apprehension pushing at him hard. When he rounded a curve, the main, sunlit canyon opened before him, shrouded in dust and gun smoke. A screaming horse wheeled, buck kicking, throwing its rider off his right rear hip, and galloping south along the stream.

In the horse's wake lay a half-dozen men, strewn as though dumped from a fast-moving wagon, twisted this way and that, hatless, inert, some lying spread-eagled over brush tufts. One man crouched behind a boulder on one knee, Winchester aimed at the ridge, smoke and flames geysering from the barrel as it bucked.

Cuno lifted his eyes to the ridge on the other side of the stream. Behind rocks and low shrubs, more smoke puffed as the gunmen there returned fire on the man crouched behind the boulder in the canyon.

Cuno's eyes creased as he shuttled his gaze from the ridge to the boulder and back again. What in blue blazes was going on?

The man behind the boulder cursed as his rifle clicked, empty. He turned his back to the rock and dropped to his butt, facing Cuno. Cuno saw the big, flat face of Brand Tuttle, blood streaming from a bullet burn on his left temple. His eyes locking on Cuno's, Tuttle's face bunched with surprise. Bunching his lips angrily, he dropped his carbine and clawed his Colt from his holster. Cuno took his time, knowing he at last had the upper hand.

He raised the carbine to his shoulder, a smile creasing his lips, and stared down the barrel. "See ye in hell, Brand."

His pistol clearing leather and extending outward, fear flashed in Tuttle's flat eyes. Cuno squeezed the carbine's trigger as Tuttle's mouth opened to yell. The stillborn words were blown back down his throat when Cuno's slug tore through the man's mouth and out the back of his head.

Tuttle jerked, stiffened, head thrown back against the boulder. His boots kicked for several seconds and gradually fell still. Tuttle toppled sideways, hitting the ground on his left shoulder. His eyes stayed locked on Cuno's, but they no longer registered a thing.

Cuno lowered the carbine and lifted his puzzled gaze to the ridge. The shooting had ceased. Smoke wafted, a haze before his eyes, curling up along the canyon walls, lit by the climbing sun.

A figure rose from behind one of the rocks on the ridge—a slender woman's figure in men's clothes complete with curl-brimmed hat, holding a rifle across her chest.

Marlene.

Four more figures rose up from rocks and shrubs, all wielding rifles. Three women and a boy wearing a bullet-crowned farm hat.

Minnie, Glory, Frieda, and Sandy. The boy waved.

Cuno shook his head, doffed his hat, and ran a sleeve across his forehead. "I'll be damned. . . ."

EPILOGUE

CUNO, THE GIRLS, and Sandy headed back to Julesburg, where Cuno holed up on Roderick's third floor, waiting for Renegade to recuperate. He was careful not to show himself on the streets. News of his fight with the Muleshoe riders had spread like wildfire, and he feared some would-be gunslick might try to make a name for himself.

One week later, when Renegade was given a clean bill of health by a knowing liveryman, Cuno and Renegade left Julesburg at dawn. He rode Renegade up a low ridge over-looking the town, and reined the horse to a halt. He studied the main thoroughfare, upon which the supply wagons and Conestogas of westering dreamers were already stirring, bull-whackers maligning their teams.

He registered little of it, however. He was thinking about Marlene. He'd said good-bye to her the day after the shoot-out, when she'd left town and ridden west along the South Platte. She'd intended to look up her aunt in Denver and settle down. Cuno felt a pang in his gut, remembering her flashing, catlike eyes, the feel of her soft lips against his when they'd parted for the last time.

"You could always ride with me to Denver," she'd said, drawing away as they stood outside the livery barn, her horse's reins in her gloved hands. "We could even"—she bit her lip wistfully and shrugged—"get hitched, if you wanted."

Cuno had only smiled at her. Deep down, they'd both known they'd gone as far as they could together.

Her eyes tearing, she threw her arms around his neck and kissed him, then wheeled, mounted her horse, and rode away. He'd watched her weave amongst the other riders and wagons until she'd disappeared among the river trees.

Cuno sighed and glanced southward, turning his thoughts to Sandy. The boy was gone now, too. He'd been taken in by a childless farm couple from south of Julesburg. His and Cuno's parting had been as hard as Cuno's and Marlene's had been. The farm couple, Josiah and Laura Adamson, were good, God-fearing people. They'd shower the boy with love and give him a solid home. Cuno had promised to write and to visit whenever he could.

Still, remembering the boy riding off in the battered old farm wagon, legs hanging over the end of the box, he felt a pang of loneliness.

The hollow loneliness was relieved when he turned his thoughts to the girls on Roderick's third floor. Last night they'd turned away their other customers, gathered in his room, and given him a parting gift he wouldn't soon forget— one, in fact, he'd probably remember on his deathbed.

He could still smell the girls' perfume, feel their gentle nibbles, feel a pair of soft supple breasts in his hands while another caressed his back. . . .

Thank God for all of them and Marlene and Sandy. He owed his life to every one of them. It had been Marlene's idea to ride out to the Muleshoe and check on him. On the trail from town, they'd spied Renegade grazing along the creek, and backtracked Cuno, approaching the ravine just as the Muleshoe riders were about to fill him with daylight.

Pinking the Muleshoe riders in that canyon had been like plucking ducks off a pond. Those whom the girls and

Sandy hadn't killed had fled, deciding that since the boss was dead, there was little point in them ending up that way, as well.

Cuno's eyes lifted over the town's salmon-washed rooftops, his smile fading now as his thoughts turned to his own future.

Where he would go, what he would do now that Evans was dead and he was no longer a hunted man, he had no idea. Not in the long run, anyway. For the moment, he intended to ride east and visit the homestead he'd only just finished building when the bounty hunters had attacked. He'd kneel at July's grave and assure her that the man responsible for her murder was dead at last.

He remembered his father and his stepmother, butchered by Rolf Anderson and Sammy Spoon back in Nebraska. He'd killed Anderson and Spoon on the Bozeman Trail, but his vengeance quest had only just begun.

Well, it was over now. His loved ones had been avenged, the bounty hunters were off his trail, and there was nothing for him to do now but find a quiet place to settle down and begin living again.

Reining Renegade off the ridge, he gigged the skewbald paint eastward, jogging along the trail over which thousands of emigrants continued traveling west. Another line of canvas-topped wagons appeared beneath the horizon, a vague outline against the climbing sun.

Meadowlarks flitted over the weeds waving along the trail, the birds' yellow breasts flashing against the sere brown of the semi-arid desert. Prairie dogs chortled as they scurried for breakfast. In the distance, shadowy, copper rimrocks humped—mysterious and hopeful.

The sun warming his face, Cuno leaned forward to give Renegade's neck an encouraging pat, then settled back in his saddle. He wasn't sure what his future held. Nonetheless, he felt at ease for the first time in a long while.

He and Renegade rode toward the dawn of a new day.

Peter Brandvold was born and raised in North Dakota. He currently resides in Colorado. His website is www.peterbrandvold.com. You can drop him an E-mail at pgbrandvold@msn.com.

PETER BRANDVOLD